DRY ICE

By

Jorge Sánchez López

A Club Lighthouse Publishing Book

ISBN: 978-1-77217-205-8

For information contact:

sales@clublighthousepublishing.com

A Club Lighthouse Mystery & Crime Edition
Published in Canada

"If only there could be
an invention that
bottled up a memory,
like scent. And it never
faded, and it never got
stale. And
then, when one wanted
it, the bottle could be
uncorked, and
it would be like living
the moment all over
again."

Daphne Du Maurier, Rebecca

"Now that you've
seen what I'm really
like, can you still bear
to look at me?"

George Orwell, 1984

APPRECIATION NOTE

To my parents, Jose and Antonia, without whom, obviously, I would not be here. To my sisters Elena and Sara and the rest of my family, which is the primary drive of life. To all of my friends and beloved beings.

To every teacher and professor who formed my way of thinking. To Manuel de Juan Espinosa, for teaching me principles of Police and Criminal Psychology many years ago.

To Ray for his useful advice, revision and training.

To the online writers' school where I gave shape to this short novel, and especially to María.

To Terrie Balmer, my editor, who thoroughly revised the manuscript, designed the cover and gave me a unique opportunity to be read at an international scale. I would also like to mention all the team, for their great artistic and social commitment.

To Pablo Molina, my great-grandparent, the writer who I couldn't meet, but whose curiosity and eagerness to express myself I seem to share.

To English Station, where I have developed professionally during the last few years.

To Lara from Virginia, for encouraging me to submit the text to North American publishers

To Jaime and Luis, editors of my previous books in Spain.

To all shop assistants, coordinators and promoters from Casa del Libro in Spain, thanks to whom I am learning a great deal about literature and talking to readers face to face.

To every reader across the globe for embarking on this project.

CHAPTER I

23 August 2018

IT IS BARELY half past six when Juan receives his wife's call. He hesitates, deciding whether to reply or not. For a number of months, their relationship had been declining. As a matter of fact, they didn't have any major conflicts. Maybe there lies the problem. Nothing happened between them. Days and weeks offered a picture which turned out to be much less exciting than he'd expected after leaving the Business School.

He finally decides to answer.

"Hi, honey. How are you?"

Adriana rushes to tell him her plan:

"I'm going to Oropesa with Malory and her husband for a week in August."

Juan didn't like the idea. *"Once again with that Irish girl?"* he thinks with a hint of distaste.

"Juan, are you there?"

He is completely absorbed with the dream catcher which hung from the rear-view mirror.

"Okay," he replies with resignation.

"It doesn't seem to please you very too much," she blurts out.

"And have you already bought the ticket? I need the car."

"She's picking me up and taking me there."

"Well, that's fine. I'm hanging up, I must drive. I'll see you in a while."

"I love you."

"See you, Darling."

He keeps his jealousy and envy firmly suppressed. He wouldn't be able to make his holidays coincide with Adriana's, as she worked in a local nursery school. Instead, he always had to beg for a week in October, another one at Christmas and the rest at the management board's discretion.

Adriana, born in Cordoba, although lacking a strong accent, had moved to El Grao, a peaceful Mediterranean coastal town where they met. They hadn't arranged a wedding ceremony, but they didn't care about that, as the marriage was formalized with the signing of documents.

Well into their thirties, they hadn't made a definitive decision about having children, which was always controversial for them.

They spent their weekends at the opera or the theatre, at restaurants, walking along the beach or strolling around shops at the shopping centre, without a precise direction.

* * * *

As soon as he's gobbled down dinner, Juan goes to his bedroom alone, thirty minutes before her. He feels tired and weak. He slowly closes his eyelids and recalls his first encounter with the Irish couple, several years back....

"Let's have lunch with a university classmate," suggested Adriana to celebrate their joining a kindergarten school where they stayed for a few months. At the bar were only a few couples and small groups of friends.

Malory proved to be a bit nosy, and he was under the impression that she talked too enthusiastically about kids, and the songs that she and Adriana used to sing with them; their daily routine. Her husband was a sweet-talker who pretended to pay attention to everything Juan and Adriana did. Anything to carry on a conversation. "Very interesting," he repeated all the time. Juan perceived the situation as a mere formality, as he was a shy person who hated socializing. Juan really valued privacy with Adriana, so he tried to enjoy quality time with her, given that he got so exhausted working as an event planner and visiting relatives on a regular basis.

Brendan, on the other hand, kept telling anecdotes about his work as an insurance salesman, in which he boasted about his excellent results. He wanted to make sure that other people's opinions about him were positive. To make matters worse, Juan despised all such displays of effusiveness; he sought to be diligent in everything he did and was polite with his friends, without falling into feigned flattery.

Everything else would have been irrelevant if he hadn't begun to notice how Adriana looked at the Irishman. He could have sworn that, with that smug attitude, he was trying to impress her and be *above everyone. They both had a gleam in their eyes that seemed suspicious.*

He never said anything to her obviously, because it never occurred to him that a girl as romantic and sensitive as Adriana would give any importance to that squirt's calls for attention. However, the frequency with which the woman went to her friends' house alone, ended up irritating him……

With his mind entangled in such memories, he falls peacefully asleep, unaware that the worst is yet to come.

CHAPTER II

31st August 2018

AT THE EDGE of the community pool, Brendan points at a group of children frolicking in the water and insulting each other. Adriana and Malory turn around and the three of them burst out laughing. Brendan looks around, checking the time on the wall clock.

"It's almost 3:30. Shall we go to the hot tub?" he suggests.

"I'm not going. I'm staying here," Adriana explains.

"Why?" Brendan asks.

"Well, you know I don't like those places. I feel terrific now that there aren't many people here. Later, if you want, we can go for a snack.

"Indeed, you're too weird," Malory laughs. "We're booked until six, but we'll probably be done by half past five. Then I'll take you to a place where they make delicious pancakes."

"I'm starting to get so hungry! Okay, have a good time."

Slightly stuttering, Lidia, the young receptionist, gives instructions to Brendan and Malory at the door of the resort. She's brunette and is wearing a Metallica tee-shirt and tight jeans.

"Please put on your flip-flops and always wear your hats on the premises."

"Sure, we've been given them before," Brendan states.

Lidia inserts the key into the lock and goes back the way she came, leaving them to their own devices. The corridors at the girls' changing rooms, where they walk around laughing like schoolchildren rejoicing at breaking the rules, lead to a spa in the middle of which there are two huge waterfalls. Malory pushes her partner, who barely manages to dive into the pool head first.

"Come on!" shouts Brendan, his back under one of the jets, his hair falling over his eyes.

Malory does the cannonball and splashes a huge volume of water.

"Aren't you ever going to learn?"

She comes over, wraps her hands around his neck and quickly kisses him on the lips. After ten minutes, Brendan suggests getting into the sauna.

"That's a drag. If you go in there, I'll wait for you in the hot tubs."

"It's very good for the respiratory system and—"

"Don't try, I'm not buying it."

"Well, I'll see you later," he announces, and then kisses her forehead.

Inside the small noisy sauna, Brendan feels the sweat running down his cheeks. He stares at the wood stove. The pores in his nose open up. Sitting on the towel, he is wrapped in the wooden structure. His body absorbs the heat from the radiation while he reflects on how lucky he is to have such a special, creative and intelligent woman by his side. Painting, music, literature, no art eludes her. Nor can he complain about her beauty. Today she shows off her spectacular curves, in that low-cut two-piece swimsuit he gave her last year. Since they're both in a good mood, they'll surely be able to have a good time and do some mischief in there. Will there be any cameras? He loves redheads with waist-length hair like her. Now that they had decided to have a baby, she'll ask the insurance company for a promotion. They'll sell the crappy apartment they bought from Gerard and move into a villa with a garden so that their future child has room to run. He's determined to convince her.

Drenched in sweat, he realizes he's lost track of time.

"What time is it now? I'm going to take a bath with Malory." He dries off and leaves the sauna. She's still in the hot tub. As soon as he sees her in the distance, he experiences a shudder that shoots up from his stomach to his throat, constricting it. He runs with numb hands, not admitting the reality of the scene.

"Malory! What's wrong with you? Malory!"

He finds her upside down; he turns her over and shakes her head from behind. Horrified by her placid smile, he feels the stiffness and the cold in her arms. On her right eye, a horrible bruise. No response.

"No! No! Help!" he screams. A choking feeling engulfs him. Nausea. As if coming out of his own body. *I'm about to die.*

Panting, he tries to leave the place, but with a misstep on the threshold, dizziness overtakes him, and he stumbles and falls. His distress call is answered by Ferran, one of the lifeguards on duty.

He's a hairy and robust man in his fifties. The guy carefully takes Brendan's pulse.

"Are you all right?"

Brendan is unable to say a word, but the terrible scene in the background confirms his misfortune. Alex, the youngest lifeguard, walks through the door, and for the first time, he finds himself in a difficult situation at work.

"What the hell is going on?" he inquires, as he sees Ferran on his knees reviving Brendan.

"Dial 112 please," the other one just says impatiently.

"But what about the woman over there?"

"We have no time to waste!"

"I don't have a phone!"

"Here, call right now!"

The boy heads for the exit. In a shaken voice, he contacts the emergency service. At the outdoor swimming pool, he is observed by many tourists. Minutes begin to feel like an eternity. He hasn't seen anything like this throughout the summer.

As Ferran steps aside, two nurses protected by self-contained breathing apparatus finally appear. They pass by, avoiding the crowd of onlookers that Alex is dealing with.

One of them, in a calm voice, gives Brendan directions to breathe; the other goes to the jacuzzi.

"My...my wife...is unconscious," he starts babbling, still unsure of his claim.

The other specialist checks that Malory's heart has stopped. Once they've got Brendan in the ambulance, several policemen from a Public Safety Patrol show up.

Gerard, the head of Helio Promotions, arrives right away, dragging his feet.

"Where is the lady?" he murmurs slowly in his slight Parisian accent, as the officers scrutinize him at the doorway.

"Are you the owner of the agency?" asks José Javier Almanzor, an inspector from the Specialized and Violent Crime Unit of the Judicial Police, where he has been investigating homicides and disappearances for five years. He is tall, dark, with a large goatee under his mask, and he's got marked cheekbones.

"That's right," Gerard answers in a slow voice.

Almanzor fixes his eyes on the Frenchman's white silk shirt. The latter scrutinizes the floating body from a distance. At the back of the room, behind the spa, the first team to gather forensic information surrounds the central hydro-massage tub.

"Please don't approach, Gerard," orders Roberto Fernández, the officer accompanying Almanzor, with a tap on the entrepreneur's shoulder. Both officers have been asked to come as additional police personnel. The area is cordoned off, waiting for the police forensics team to come and take fingerprints before the body is lifted.

The manager looks both ways, confused.

"Who's in charge of maintenance?" nags Jose Javier. He looks at the woman, enveloped by a cloud of carbonic snow. Not a single scratch...." the word suspended on her lips, or so he imagines. Every sign points to choking.

Three men are taking pictures from different angles. The body is leaning over with outstretched arms.

Gerard is tongue-tied.

"It's a company called Gris".

"Just Gris?" Roberto objects. He means to ask something else.

"Do you have the phone?" Almanzor inquires, anticipating events.

They clear out all the rooms and the pool. Adriana, the couple's friend, is asked to stay away too. The cameras crowd the circle of foamy water again. Two members of the patrol take notes and sketch the scene.

"The lady drowned while her husband was in the sauna," explains Almanzor.

"But that's impossible! The water isn't deep enough for her to drown in!

"What was in the water?" Adriana wails. She feels a heavy constriction in her chest.

"We're not sure. We'll know when we get the forensic report. I'm very sorry about what happened to your friend, but you have to leave. Give me your number and we'll keep you informed."

"Please, let me enter." She's breathing heavily, visibly distressed.

With intense pressure in her throat and stomach, she unsuccessfully attempts to convince the policeman to allow her to see Malory, constantly repeating the same request. In the end, Roberto takes her by the arm and guides her to the back door. After vacating the common pool area, the officer goes to the reception, where he demands that a group of people take the elevator in an orderly fashion and return to their homes. On the street the noise is obvious, although some remain in their vehicles, waiting for further orders.

* * * *

A NURSE TAKES Brendan's blood pressure inside the emergency room of Oropesa hospital. He continues to hyperventilate. Another one administers 1 milligram of Lorazepam. He insists on notifying his entire family in Dublin.

"As soon as you're better," they tell him. If necessary, they'll do it for him.

"Why didn't I go in with her?" he desperately laments. "Malory doesn't find saunas amusing."

The nurse brings him the phone. Still feeling a tingling in his limbs, he makes an effort to get it closer to his ear.

A deep voice wakes him up:

"I'm José Javier Almanzor, national police inspector."

"What... What did you find out?"

"We're sorry to inform you that your wife has passed away."

Brendan is slow to react.

"No! No!" His hoarse voice is drowning in the air.

"We're really sorry. We'll need you. If you'll be so kind, come and give evidence as soon as you're better. They'll probably call you tomorrow."

Shortly after, he's taken upstairs to an assigned room, he is informed that he'll be kept overnight for observation.

* * * *

ADRIANA, STILL NOT believing what happened, calls Juan, who answers after a couple of rings.

"Juan! Something terrible has happened!"

"What? Don't scare me. What is it?"

"Malory's dead!" she shrieks breathlessly.

"What?"

"She turned up dead in the hot tub. They don't know why! I'm so unsettled."

"She had a heart attack?"

"I don't know. I don't know. I'll have to testify later. I'll be there this afternoon."

"Are you sure?" He bites his upper lip, while rubbing his chin on the phone.

"Yes, yes, as soon as I calm down, I'll set off."

"Calm down, we'll talk. I love you."

It's an hour's drive, at least for someone like Adriana, who's not known for being a speed freak.

When Juan comes in, she's already waiting for him in the armchair, distraught and unable to move. After hugging her, he tries hopelessly to comfort her with caresses. During dinner, the man thinks about the damn time she decided to go on holiday with her friends, but says absolutely nothing. She reluctantly agrees to eat some sausage and a couple of pieces of fruit, which she has a hard time swallowing, while she gives details the scene. He listens intently, watching her face, but shows no surprise.

Tired, Adriana goes to bed, this time before Juan. She needs to gather strength to deal with the many children at the nursery school where she works. Although she only manages to get two hours of sleep, she arrives at work at half past seven on the dot.

CHAPTER III

José Javier Almanzor

September 2, 2018- Jaume I University

"DOES ANYONE HAVE any questions...? Yes, the difference between the behavioural activation system and the inhibition system, is that the former is used in order to obtain a reward: money, work, sex, whatever. The second one... the second one is based on the avoidance of punishment. For example, the child who doesn't dare to be late coming home in case he gets an earful. Both systems function abnormally in the case of certain offenders, who have either too high an activation or too low an inhibition. Okay? Any more questions? No? Well, we're running out of time. If you're going to train as criminologists, you'll need to steel yourself for it. I know that many of you have signed up out of morbid curiosity. In one of my classes last year, I had a student who got dizzy because we played a video about a baby's murder. If anyone is uncomfortable and can't continue, please tell me: 'Hey, Jose Javier, I'm really screwed up about this'. You might want to be like Clarice Starling and when there's a murderer you can raffle him off. But frankly, this is a long-distance race and you're not bound to get medals just like that. OK? All right, see you next time, that's it for today, remember I'm in my office for tutoring on Wednesdays at 11.30."

Almanzor leaves the classroom quickly when he notices his mobile vibrating in the pocket of his jacket. He checks and sees that it's his boss, commissioner Isabel Camacho, who's calling from Castellón.

"Hi, what's new?"

"We've been giving Malory's case serious consideration and we want you to take it over."

The subordinate sighs and scratches his left temple.

"Isn't there another one to screw around with?"

"Almanzor, you were the one who complained that you had a lot of tasks but were stuck. There's no one better than you for this."

He remains silent for a few seconds before accepting.

"Why not?"

"Well, a dubious murder case. According to the preliminary study, there are no prints. All psychology. You're the expert."

He knows that, when Isabel talks this way, there's no ironic intent in her statements.

"And what about the classes?"

"No problem. Tell the department coordinator you need a leave of absence urgently. You just made the presentation, didn't you?"

"Okay, I'll think about it."

"There's nothing to think about. Tomorrow you'll have Brendan and, in the afternoon, the Frenchman from the agency. Interview them and, when you're done, we'll talk about the meetings."

"All right, Isabel, see you tomorrow," he says a solemn farewell.

* * * *

WITH HIS MIND still on the new assignment, he wanders around the car park looking for his semi-new Opel Corsa. As soon as she finds it, he starts up and presses the accelerator firmly. In less than half an hour, he shows up at her house, kisses Sonia and little Izan and sprawls out on the sofa.

"What's up? What about the Jacuzzi?" Sonia asks.

"I've been given it," he says reluctantly. However, he realizes the enthusiasm that his news provokes.

"Well, is that so bad? You'll do great. Won't he, Izan?"

The kid nods. "Yeah, great. What a hard job. Have you started school, Dad?" the boy asks fascinated, even more so than usual, since he's a few days away from starting the first grade of primary school." The father smiles.

"Yes, but another teacher will help me. I'll be too busy chasing after the bad guys."

Izan looks at the man from top to bottom. He spins a stuffed cube with his hands.

"Like in the Batman cartoons?"

"Same thing, son, but being more handsome."

Then the three of them look at each other and burst out laughing.

CHAPTER IV

BRENDAN COMES TO the station on his own. He identifies himself at the entrance to a young policeman, who searches him after going through the metal detector. The two bodies are well toned, although it could be said that being a forty-year-old, the Irish man can boast a larger biceps and higher shoulder width. Once the process has been completed, he is accommodated by a gray-haired sub-inspector in the waiting room, where a teenager narrates to his parents, probably for the umpteenth time, the theft of his wallet containing money and documentation.

In two minutes, an officer asks him to go to the back. There, after noticing the squeaking sound of the door, he meets Almanzor, standing in a firm position and with a severe expression. On the right, Roberto goes over to a mountain of papers on his seat.

"Good morning, Brendan. Sit down," the inspector orders. "As we told you on the phone, we have a warrant," he says.

"Am I going to stay here?" Brendan babbles.

"We need you to make a statement. You'll spend the day under arrest. You have the right to remain silent. Anything you say can be used against you in a court of law. You have the right to an attorney. If you cannot afford it, one will be appointed for you. Tomorrow you'll be brought to court to testify. Do you understand?"

Disgruntled, Brendan holds his shaky hands over his identity card. As required, he takes off his belt and delicately puts his wallet, keys and mobile phone on the table. Almanzor then begins to ask questions, while Roberto prepares to write on the keyboard.

"Tell me, how did all this happen?"

Brendan takes a deep breath and watches the agent cross his arms.

"My wife and I booked the facilities for the 31st, Thursday," he explains in a gruff way. At about four in the afternoon, we took a bath for about ten minutes at the spa. Then Malory stayed in one of the three hot tubs, the one downtown. I went into one of the saunas for half an hour, more or less. She didn't want all that heat. On the way out, I saw her lying on her back. She didn't respond no matter how hard I tried to wake her up. That's when I collapsed, and the lifeguards called 112."

"Why did you go into the sauna alone?"

"She doesn't like it, but it's useful for eliminating toxins and improving circulation."

Because of his eloquence of speech, Almanzor thinks of a possible tendency to show his intelligence to others and get away with it. His restlessness, however, doesn't correspond to a cold personality capable of committing a crime without flinching.

"Did you touch her?"

"Yes, I got in the water and dragged her to the surface. I gave her mouth-to-mouth, but she wouldn't move. The lifeguard came running to help me," says Brendan waving his forearms.

"What may have happened is that your wife was intoxicated. There was an excess of dry ice-solid carbon dioxide that turns to gas without passing through the liquid state— In principle it's not toxic, but in high concentrations it can cause death. Maybe it was mixed with other substances." Almanzor explains.

"How could that be? I don't understand."

"Forensics are analyzing the scene."

Your friend Adriana wasn't with you?" interrupts Roberto, observing the Irishman's inappropriate flower shirt.

"She didn't feel like coming, said she'd rather leave us alone."

"Do you know where she stayed?" asks the officer.

"Yes, in the swimming pool."

"Who could have brought the ice in?"

"I don't know, I have no idea," he shrugs.

Roberto and the inspector look at each other with furrowed brows.

"You must bear in mind that, although it's not entirely certain, if a company error is ruled out, the clues point to intoxication," asserts Almanzor, with a penetrating stare at Brendan, designed to unnerve him.

"Hey? What are you implying? You don't think that I did it, do you? Those scumbags will pay for what they've done!" he yells.

"Don't shout or threaten anyone. We're very sorry for your wife, but we don't claim anything. For the moment, we have no choice but to keep you in custody until tomorrow. It's a mandatory procedure.

Have you ever been in the dungeon?" the inspector asks.

The two policemen see that his legs are shaking.

"Well...Once, for driving at 170, about two hours. It was a long time ago," he whispers.

"How long?" demands Roberto.

"Five years, when we moved here. The road was 120. I haven't done it ever since."

"Where did you meet?" suddenly asks Almanzor.

"What difference does it make? At a party with some friends. We went to Phoenix Park, a big one in Dublin, and then to a disco."

"I know it, I've travelled a lot," claims José Javier, trying to empathise. Definitely a beautiful place... Are you married?

"Yes, we celebrated the wedding in Ireland and then we came here a little over three years ago."

"Okay, and what do you do? "

"I'm an insurance salesman. Malory works, she worked" – it hurts him to use the past tense – in a child centre. We were going to have a fucking child!"

His eyes become red, and he breaks down in tears.

"I'm really sorry. I understand your pain because I'm a father. The more information we have, the sooner it will be solved. What's your relationship with your sister-in-law, Mrs. Eileen? We know she lives here, right?"

"I have a sixteen-year-old niece, whose name is Sinead. We get on well. We usually visit her on Sundays" he realizes he's using the present this time.

"All right, that's enough for now. Take off your shoelaces. When you're done, go to the back room."

The dungeon is a dark room where Brendan sits on a wooden bench, much cooler than the jacuzzi. Fate has shown him its most rotten face. On the wall, several names and aliases have been scratched with a sharp object: Sarri, Pablo, César, Marquitos, Pitu. Inside the office, Almanzor drinks black coffee and instructs Roberto to check the police records, while he reviews the crime photos for anything unusual. He pauses and provides the detainee in the cell with a sandwich, water and some cookies with the police force's shield on the wrapper.

"Indeed, we mistreat you," he jokes. "You know? Nobody makes the sandwiches like we do here."

The other one looks at him in confusion. Almanzor locks the door again and then prepares to phone Gerard.

"Who is it?"

"Good morning, Gerard Briand?"

"Yeah, speaking."

"I'm Inspector José Javier Almanzor, I'm calling from Oropesa del Mar police station. I need you to come here, so that I can ask you some questions," he says in a relaxed voice.

"Oh, yes, all right."

The experienced inspector can guess his desire to hide his nervousness.

"Come at four o'clock" he firmly orders Gerard.

CHAPTER V

IN FRONT OF the entrance to the police station, Gerard repeats to himself that he doesn't have anything to hide, but he is uncomfortable with being splashed by a scandal like that, which may end up on television. He now hopes to tell the police and the judges, as if making it clear only once, was not enough. He promises himself that he'll maintain his personal and professional reputation as he fits his tie before going up the access ramp.

Brendan is still locked in the dungeon. Since Almanzor has made sure to keep safe the copies of the photos provided by forensics, the office looks the same as it did when Malory's husband was questioned: tidy, but with two mountains of papers next to the computer.

When he shakes hands with the real estate developer, the inspector checks that the other one's applying the expected firmness. He notices that not only has the Frenchman replaced his ring, but also the finger on which he wears it, which means that he is a luxury-loving married man. In front of Gerard, Roberto finishes typing some data into the computer. Then he gets up, greets him and invites him to sit down.

"Well, Gerard, provide some proof of identity," he adds.

The passport says that Gerard Briand Bélanger is fifty-two years old. The officer is surprised: despite his baldness, he doesn't look his age, given his lack of wrinkles.

Almanzor remains silent for a moment before explaining:

"It seems that the mechanical parts of the Jacuzzi have no fault. Everything indicates that there's an excess of dry ice. Did you talk to the company's workers on the day of the... accident?"

Although he's certain that it was provoked, he prefers not to employ an inappropriate strategy that may arouse undue suspicion in the inspector. The Frenchman scratches his head, as if remembering.

"Not personally. I'm in real estate. The employees deliver material on a regular basis. I know they'd filled in the shipping note of a 25 kg box the day before, but they don't need to ask me for

permission about it."

"Who was at the reception desk?"

"I suppose it was Lidia, the girl who works the morning shift."

"Suppose?" Almanzor gives him a sour look.

"She left at twelve to go to a doctor's appointment, and Francisco took her place during that interval, but the report specifies that it was ten thirty. I'm not sure who brought the material."

"We'll check it out. And who has the keys to the Jacuzzi?"

"Lidia herself, who allowed them to access. She has a copy. The other one is in my office, in case there's a loss. They had it reserved from three thirty to six."

"Was there anyone in the pool?"

"Yeah, Alex, the lifeguard."

"Do you think someone might have tried to hurt him?"

Despite his long experience, Almanzor needs to ask that naive question, because the chilling thing about the case is precisely the impossibility of determining whether it was a simple and macabre trackless murder, without any marks or blood, or rather an irresponsible act shared by the maintenance company and the agency. Did anyone else come in within that time frame, husband and wife each being in a different corner?

"She was quite peaceful, had no enemies."

"What else can you tell us about the deceased?"

"She lived in one of the flats."

"Which one?" Robert interjects.

"Room 101."

"How long had she been there?"

"Seven years. I sold it to her myself. There were good promotions back then."

"Were you on good terms with her?"

"As a landlord, I used to confine myself to solving her maintenance problems. I called in the right professionals. Other times I'd put her in touch with realtors. She was the one who used to approach me first."

"And the husband?"

"Brendan and me, we barely spoke, except when he walked her into my office. It was always Malory who consulted me."

"What do you reckon their relationship was like?" Almanzor redirects the conversation.

"Apparently, they made a lovely couple. They'd been living together in Ireland for three years by the time they arrived."

"And Adriana, the woman they had as a guest?"

"I'd seen her before, a couple of summers ago. You know that the locals live here intermingle with their tourists, and that there are tenants who rent only in holiday periods. It is in summer and at Easter when they do – more often..."

"Do you suspect someone they might have as an enemy?" Roberto breaks in gently.

"I have no idea. Sorry, I don't know much more." Gerard lies.

"What about the lifeguards? Can't they provide any information?" Almanzor insists.

"I honestly don't think so. They don't have access to the jacuzzi."

Inspector Almanzor drums his fingers on the table. Preparing the next move, he looks down for a few moments and says:

"Alright, thanks for your help. We'll need you to come back soon. Please let us know anything that comes to your attention. Your cooperation is indispensable."

"Sure, it'll be a pleasure."

"You can go now."

Almanzor realizes that the Frenchman is breathing heavily: it looks like he's going to choke. Nevertheless, he gets up dragging his chair and leaves the room almost without looking, quickly waving goodbye before heading for the door.

José Javier takes a look at his assistant's face, and without assessing what has happened, gives him instructions:

"Roberto, stay here and accompany him to the courthouse tomorrow. Another agent will go with you. Tonight I'm going to talk with Commissioner Camacho and with Rosa and Inés, from the forensic team."

"Hey, Jose...." he finds himself calling him by his first name... "Do you think this Gerard is hiding something?"

"Obviously he's not stupid, but I don't know... He's not made for murdering a woman."

"You've got weird ideas."

"Maybe...Well, we'll see each other tomorrow afternoon."

Almanzor bids farewell, patting him on the shoulder.

With his usual seriousness, Roberto comes in to bring dinner to Brendan. A tortilla sandwich and a bottle of mineral water.

"There you go. I'm terribly sorry about what happened to your wife."

"Thank you very much. I still can't believe she's dead. Oh, my God!"

"I understand you, mine died of a tumor a year ago."

"Damn, I'm so sorry."

Suddenly, cries in Arabic and banging bars are heard in an adjacent cell. Roberto takes on his most commanding tone to bring order.

Recalling his own key life events, Brendan witnesses a kaleidoscopic procession of images. His reputation as captain of the rugby team is no use to him, handcuffed as he is.

That party with his colleagues from work, which was joined by Administration and Management students. He recovers the moment he saw Malory arrive. It must have been one of the girls from Politics who introduced him to her, but he has a vague memory of who did it. Her shyness when he asked her out, their long walks in the park, the first kiss, the first fuck, the house they rented in Ireland. Then come the laughs shared when Brendan, whose mother is a Spaniard, used to help Malory perfect her Spanish. Their desire to move to Spain. The trip.

It seems unbelievable that, being so sociable, she can't now respond to all those scientists she provides with entertainment. For them she's nothing but a mere resource to fatten their academic ego. A cloud of unreality catches her. Unfortunately, he isn't dreaming: the nightmare takes shape in her existence...

Sleepless, he's mentally reviewing pending tasks. Yesterday he called his parents, who after expressing their condolences and gathering the small amount of information he could provide, told him that his brother Trevor had left the detoxification center. Frankly, he didn't give a damn. They also begged him to return to his native country. He wasn't going to do it until he learnt what miserable rat had hurt Malory.

So, he still needs to talk to Eileen and Adriana. Remembering that he has several missing calls from both of them, he rests his arms on his bent knees. Meanwhile, he ponders how he'll confess that he's been arrested. As soon as the police release him, he will take the Nissan in the direction of the funeral home.

At eight o'clock, without having slept, he is given a cup of coffee with two muffins by Roberto. Brendan collects his belongings and then is handcuffed and transported to the van, under the scrutiny of those queuing to renew their identity cards.

Roberto and another strong policeman who is about to retire, take him to court. Once there, he repeats his statement to a lawyer with big round glasses and a stone-cold face. A law clerk prints the report. It has always seemed to Brendan that these types of individuals misinterpret other people's words when they write. He's handed in the paper, which he keeps in his pocket. Before leaving, he exchanges a few words with the public defender, Mr. Rois, assuring him that he isn't guilty. The Irishman takes the attorney's business card and leaves.

The gentle end-of-summer breeze doesn't relax him as much as he'd expect under other circumstances. On his way home, he makes the appropriate calls. Although Adriana's number comes first alphabetically in the directory, he dials Eileen's first. After three rings she answers.

"Brendan, sweetie. What happened? I've been calling you. Have you been discharged yet?"

"Eileen! Sorry, I haven't been able to phone. Yeah, I'm out. I'm so upset. I don't... I don't know. She couldn't get out of the water! I went into the sauna, I..."

For a moment he is relieved that Eileen didn't stay overnight in the hospital, as she would have discovered the subsequent proceedings and his arrest. Brendan had been taken to hospital after suffering a panic attack, and from there is phoning his sister-in-law Eileen about Malory's death.

"My dear little sister. At only thirty-five years of age," Eileen whispers." No, it is not your fault."

"They threw a load of dry ice in the hot tubs. She fell down, because there was this bump on her head. It must be some son of a bitch from that company who is to blame. Either it was on purpose or they're useless. They're gonna pay for what they've done."

"They'll get caught, for sure." Eileen sympathises with him.

Brendan takes a short break.

"Are you home? Do you know when they're taking her to the mortuary?"

"They haven't told us yet."

"They agreed to call me in the morning too. How's Sinead?"

"Well, here she is, sitting on the sofa, shattered, crying... Sinead, do you want to talk to your uncle? She can't do it right now. We'd better meet at the funeral. I love you, Brendan."

"So do I. Kisses."

He hangs up and tries to reach Adriana. Even though it shows a signal, she doesn't pick it up. She must be busy. He doesn't keep her husband's or their home number, so as soon as he gets to the apartment he lays down in bed, head on his knees, waiting for the news, so as to attend the wake.

CHAPTER VI

Through the balcony, Izan, Almanor's son, is distracted by the cars passing in both directions. His father takes a sip of the coffee and looks at Sonia, who shows him a newspaper with a satisfied look.

"Have you seen this? It's badly written.

"What's the matter with it, teacher?" he shrugs.

"It says, "The Irish woman who died in Oropesa would have been allegedly poisoned. For a rumour, the correct way is "might have been poisoned."

"Yeah, that's so awkward."

Izan suddenly turns his head.

"What does "poisoned" mean? Has poison been poured into her coffee?"

The inspector looks at his wife, with a "you could have shut up" look on his face. He considers how many arguments with colleagues he'll get into if he defends that hypothesis.

"Well, it's not that. She took a bath in a pool full of toxic ice."

"And why?"

"We don't know who poured the thing into it, nor if she even noticed, son. People do very silly things sometimes."

The watch on Almanor's wrist—an unusual device these days—tells him it's time to leave. Once in the car, he waves to Sonia and Izan, who send him off shouting happily from above.

On the road, he ponders the unusual nature of the case. Could Izan be right? Was she drugged? Did she suffer from any previous pathologies? He also asks himself: Was this what I wanted in the end? He reflects on his hypothetical ability to adapt to Europol, where his prestige would increase by joining international groups. He could also be part of the GEOs, which might allow him to participate in high-risk operations. He infers that there is a reason to continue investigating murders and disappearances that eludes him. If that distant cousin of his mother's had not been dismembered when he was a child, he would not have developed such an interest in criminology. Far from being the result of a trauma like the one typically suffered by detectives in the movies, his professional choice is more like destiny.

The facade of the Legal Medicine and Forensic Anatomical Institute of Castellón, located in Argentina Street, always reminds him of the courts of Madrid. He passes by two parked bicycles and goes to the main door, where he finds two men with sunglasses who are smoking. Almanzor congratulates himself on having kicked the habit.

He climbs the stairs at a fast pace and heads for the autopsy room. Commissioner Isabel Camacho is with Rosa, a specialist in remains and cybercrime from the National Police. They greet him five metres away from the corpse.

In the background, Malory's body is measured, weighed, carelessly transported—in Almanzor's opinion—and finally lain on the stretcher by the pathologists. Sweat samples are taken and all organs are washed. The sclera of her eyes is surrounded by a red rim produced by chlorine. In addition to the bruise on her cheekbone, she has two burns on her belly and a blister on her left arm due to frostbite.

Inés Muñoz, the forensic pathologist, makes a Y-shaped cut on the chest. Inspector Almanzor, given the silence of his colleagues, concentrates on the operation and reflects on it.

When it seems that the dead speak, it is reality that strikes us with its unanswered questions. The label attached to the foot is not going to give the girl, or better still the woman, her humanity back. The freshness of a life she has lost at the tender age of thirty-five. After all, where does dignity go when you leave this insane world behind?

Moderating her tone of voice, Rosa finally decides to speak.

"At the jacuzzi there is a sign indicating that it's closed until further notice. Every machine has been analyzed, including the one responsible for the fatality. No mechanical failure has occurred. Dry ice, an eloquent metaphor for criminal awareness."

"The natural state is gaseous", José Javier mumbles. Isabel is not so sure.

"What we need to see is whether we're dealing with a murderer, or just negligence attributable to a company."

"Roberto will give us some clues" Almanzor declares in an eclectic manner. He still thinks it's a murder.

"I want you to see what Brendan emailed us." Isabel changes the subject.

The three visitors gather around the table where a pile of photos of Malory can be seen. In one of them she appears much younger, wearing the cap and gown at the graduation ceremony for Early Childhood Education teachers at Trinity College. Almanzor slips it between his fingers eagerly. He comes across another image where the girl poses on the beach with her sister Eileen and the latter's Argentine ex-husband, who died in a boating accident, just as Brendan told Rosa by email.

After passing two more snapshots of Malory making out with Brendan in the centre of Dublin, and one in which she smiles at the camera from the back row of what appears to be a group of Erasmus students, he finally sees it. The girl, unaware of the camera, dances in a nightclub. Her two friends catch the photographer's eye. The inspector identifies Adriana, whom he sent home on the day of the crime, along with a Colombian woman.

"That disco is in Oropesa," he points out. He looks for confirmation.

"It's Palm Trees Nightclub. Brendan says it's been operating for about three years," says Rosa.

"How can this help?"

"I have no idea, but you need to question those two girls. Rosa, Brendan told you that Adriana came regularly to visit the couple, didn't she? The other one is called Daniela and lives in the residential area," says Isabel.

Rosa keeps quiet. She seethes with anger because, once again, the boss has ignored her by answering instead of her.

"In which street?" says Almanzor.

Isabel adopts an ironic tone.

"Ask Gerard if you have time to spare."

At that moment, Ines approaches and greets José Javier, who pries into her findings. Patronizingly, because she is known to be the most scientifically qualified, the coroner points out;

"The analysis of the temperature of the organs indicates that Malory died within a few minutes. It seems clear that the material had to be introduced the day before. There are no other toxic substances."

"I don't like how it sounds" Rosa intervenes.

"Her skin colour confirms asphyxiation," Inés announces. "It was very pale and now it's red, but there's no sign of violence. We can't say much more. This evidence would allow us to rule out any struggle with her husband, if it weren't for how she hit her head. She may have been dizzy and fallen on her back when she tried to dive back into the water."

"Where's the blow?"

Ines shows him the capture they just took.

"Maybe he did that, or rather it was someone who came in unseen and threw her to the ground" Rosa speculates.

"But you should think that, as Ines says, perhaps he swam in two of the Jacuzzis," suggests Isabel, who never categorically asserts any theory is true, at least in front of her subordinates. "One of them also contains an excess of dry ice. The third, nothing. Breathing in all that invisible fog and losing consciousness, she perhaps crashed headlong into the edge of the central one."

Almanzor, who doesn't want to lose prominence, even if it's only to convey the uncertainty that invades him, categorically proves himself to be right.

"Judicial experts are analyzing air samples, as well as checking all the facilities. They have cleaned the room because there was an excess concentration of CO_2 and smoke. The Jacuzzi has been closed until further notice."

The commissioner, stunned, hears him spouting the obvious in front of the coroner.

"Well, this is it. Almanzor, talk to Roberto. Tell me what they say in Gris, the maintenance company, and then you two must go to the wake. See you at the funeral" she concludes, pointing at the door with her index finger.

The viscera and the brain are removed, examined and repositioned by the experts. The wounds are closed, but the debacle hovers over a wide area.

CHAPTER VII

On THE PROMENADE where Almanzor has arranged to pick up Roberto as soon as he exchanges his police car for his Opel, the lights on the terraces attract the first customers of the night. *"I wish I could take a dip,"* he thinks longingly, stuffed into his jacket and black pants, staring at the desert sea caressed by the dunes.

"Sorry for the delay," Roberto apologizes as he opens the passenger door.

"How did it go? Let's go to the morgue, for a short while. That should be enough."

"Well, first I talked to Lidia at the reception and then I went to Gris. They seem to follow clear-cut protocols. The company has worked together with Promociones Helio to obtain an ISO 9001 certification for sports and leisure facilities. Both the Jacuzzi and the swimming pool were audited earlier this year. The workers don't look suspicious. They also arrange all kinds of performances, focusing on sound, image and atmospheric special effects at a disco in Benicàssim, where Gerard's brother also works."

"Who did you talk to at Gris?" insists Roberto. Almanzor stops the car at a traffic light near the town center ring road.

"The boss, Ariel. He was quite friendly to me. He took me to an office with one Fran, who according to Lidia, the receptionist, is a friend of hers. He was one of the two who took the box to the hotel."

"Fuck, and you don't find that suspicious? Besides, it's not a hotel, Roberto, it's an apartment block," says Almanzor.

"Well, whatever. After all, tourists are mixed with residents. The thing is, Lidia took the register around 10:15. She says there were two of them dressed in uniforms. She put the dry ice in the Jacuzzi the very day of the accident."

"You call it that way too? let's see what Rosa says, but there was over twice **more** carbonic snow than usual."

Roberto's face is clouded with an angry frown.

"Dry ice is not indispensable, it's almost decorative. Anyone who works there knows how to chlorinate and change the water. I have the recording showing Lidia carrying exactly a 25kg box. By the way, she's really hot. There's another video from the day before, but I skimmed through the recording quickly and there isn't anybody."

"Man, you're such a pervert," says Almanzor smiling. "They have close circuit television, don't they?"

"Yeah, but it doesn't reach the Jacuzzi because it's a private area. They installed it only at the entrance, in case someone breaks in.

Almanzor watches him skeptically as they approach the parking lot of the mortuary building, where he tries to find a parking space. He remembers out loud that the only time he has seen that mortuary, was on television a few years ago, when they covered the case of a South American woman who was raped and murdered.

"I can't forget that," says Roberto. "The culprit is serving his sentence here in the capital. A disturbed man from Castellón."

Seeing a Skoda who has just taken his place, the inspector repeatedly honks his horn. Inside he sees a man making a fuss.

"What are you doing, you idiot?" Almanzor shrieks with the window closed, stopping the car aside.

He parks in another row and looks for the man, but he has already left. The room where the wake takes place is on the first floor. Behind the burial chamber, in front of two empty leather sofas, Roberto contemplates Malory, stiff in a supine position.

"What if she killed herself?" he whispers in his comrade's ear.

"Come on, don't stay here," says Almanzor, noticing the man watching from the back sofa. To his surprise, the same man he scolded in the parking lot. He's ashamed of himself when he realizes that the blonde woman next door, her hands on her thighs and tragedy tattooed on her face, is Adriana.

Without even opening her mouth, she crosses paths with Eileen and her daughter, who are just as Brendan had described them. They are crying in each other's arms.

"Excuse me, I'm Inspector Almanzor, sorry for your loss."

He admits to himself that this is a sensitive moment, but he knows that if he moderates his verbosity, he will be able to summon the mother to testify. If he assures her that he is committed to working hard to find out what happened to Malory, he might easily get her cooperation after a few days. By the time he expands his visual scope, Adriana's companion has already left. Almanzor approaches her with a gentle step and speaks to her, whispering.

"Night, Adriana. I'm so sorry."

"Thank you very much."

"Excuse me, where's the man who was with you?"

"Juan, my husband?"

"Yes. Sorry, but I got nervous, I honked the horn and..."

"Don't worry, he's very stubborn. He just went to look for the toilets. This place is very big, you know?"

Roberto clears his throat to get the inspector's attention and then walks off to greet the rest of the people. Almanzor turns around, nods his head and remains waiting at the same place. He sees Juan arrive with his hands in his pockets and rushes to talk to him.

"Good night. I'm sorry I got impatient at..."

Suddenly, Juan's face changes; the policeman looks more reasonable to him than before.

"It doesn't matter, you must be under a lot of stress."

Almanzor says goodbye and joins his subordinate in expressing his condolences to those who happen to be Malory's parents, who remain prostrate on another of the couches. He assumes that they have come from Ireland on a last-minute flight. The scene is completed by two Colombians, Daniela and Anthony, accompanied by their daughter Edith, who after introducing herself only listens to the conversation. Almanzor recognises the mother, one of those posing in the disco photo, slightly fatter and with shorter hair. The husband, who must be in his forties, is tall and slender, with gelled hair and a gold chain around his neck.

Soon someone points out that it's eleven o'clock and the cops ride down in the elevator with Anthony, Daniela and Edith. Only Malory's family members, Juan and Adriana, are left. The latter seems to be trying to contain Juan's anger when she says she wants to watch her friend all night.

The agents can't believe their eyes. "Beware," reads the graffiti on the side of the Opel. Under the windshield wiper a cell phone number has been written down. As soon as he realizes that his tires have been punctured, Almanzor's anger merges with fear.

"What are they playing at?" snarls Roberto, who complains that he will get home late, which annoys him even though he doesn't have to justify himself to anyone.

"You can go, Roberto. I'll stay and call the tow-truck," says Almanzor. Although he can imagine a certain disgruntled gesture from Sonia, he always tries to set an example.

"Shall I drive you home, officer?" Anthony asks.

"Thank you very much, but I'm staying," Roberto decides.

"Can we have your phone numbers? After the funeral, we'd like you to come to the police station and tell us everything you know about your friend. The more we find out, the sooner we'll catch the perpetrator," says Almanzor.

The family moves through the different rows towards their car. The inspector dials the number on the paper several times, but it is dead. Controlling his anxiety, he phones Isabel to inform her of the facts.

"Okay, we'll check who it belongs to. I want you to be very attentive at the funeral, OK?" the inspector orders without getting too concerned.

* * * *

THE NEXT DAY, after the request for forgiveness and the Rite of Light, the priest begins his prayer:

We pray, Lord, for Malory Byrne O'Neill, who was so close and dear to us, and for that reason we have gathered together with her. Grant her the happy and joyful life she so desired; and grant us the strength to continue to be united among ourselves and with You, to fulfill our simple daily duties as persons and as Christians. We ask this through Jesus Christ our Lord.

The faces are practically the same, with the exception of Gerard and three friends of Sinead's, who must have come out of sheer commitment. The parish, located in the centre of the town, is not much larger than one would expect, although it is certainly the right place to honour a parishioner like Malory, a regular at Mass without exception.

Because of his closeness to her, the speaker adds to the sermon a reference to some of the qualities of the deceased. In this case, quite rightly, he underlines her dedication to others and her kind nature, as well as the gleams she used to have in her eye.

Almanzor and Roberto walk ahead of the rest, back to the car, as soon as the funeral is over. It begins to rain heavily. The inspector switches on his cell phone and checks that he has several missed calls from Rosa.

"Morning, José Javier."

He finds it strange that she calls him by his name, not so much because of the lack of habit but because it bothers him that a forensic expert in cybercrime occasionally speaks to him that way.

"What have we got?"

"The phone's been disconnected. We've obtained court permission to trace it. It belongs to Alex, the lifeguard."

"Did you manage to locate the boy?"

"Yeah. He seemed quiet. He swears he didn't do the graffiti and he has no idea who might have incriminated him. He says there are some kids who've been wanting to hit him for a while. I've already spoken to the municipal police force at Benicàssim, where he's moved. You can question him this afternoon.

Almanzor takes note of the boy's identity card and new phone number. He watches the windshield wiper move frantically before setting off on the wet road.

Finally, he asks Roberto to make an appointment with Adriana, who lives in El Grao, a nearby town. In turn, Almanzor himself will question Alex. Then he keeps silent for most of the trip.

In his long career in crime, having worked on several patrols and collaborated on the most sordid cases, Almanzor hasn't come across one so disturbing or complex, a sweet death with hardly any traces, the most puzzling crime, however, apparently harmless, that an inspector can encounter. Both his work and that of scientists is bound to consist of many layers, adding the efforts of judges, lawyers and journalists, these so keen on gossip. "Public opinion is sure to do the rest," he thinks. It's only a matter of time before the town is empty, as it has already been blacklisted by many tourists, which is noticeable in the few visitors who come as compared to previous years.

CHAPTER VIII

ADRIANA FEELS SHE'S being strangled by her own thoughts. The children's laughter and tears are fading. She begins to walk with no apparent purpose.

She doesn't identify the classrooms, where songs are heard, the closed office of the director or the empty reception desk. Repeated knocking on the door echoes behind her. Without knowing why, she turns around and runs away towards the exit then notices the rain in the street. It's getting late and she has to do something important, so she crosses at the traffic light so quickly, jumping through the puddles, her red sweater is soaking wet. She boards the first bus that passes by and stands in the middle of the crowd, like a ghost.

She wants to call her business partner, but she realizes that her phone is not in her pocket, so she waits until the last stop. On the monitor it says "Oropesa". The other passengers get out and the driver approaches her tentatively.

"Everything okay?"

"Yeah, yeah, sorry." Distractedly, she gets off and walks between blocks of flats. At the circus they're advertising a comic show. She wanders down the street, passing by a real estate agency called Promociones Helio and by a block of flats behind which she sees people swimming in the pools, which makes her slightly nervous.

She ends up in a bar where there are only four old people playing a Spanish card game and drinking hot chocolate.

The bartender, a young dark-haired boy with the name 'Derek' on his name tag, approaches her. He is broad-shouldered and has greasy hair.

"Are you ready to order?"

Adriana is slow to answer.

"A green tea, please."

"Something to eat, ma'am?"

She then thinks of her own age, which he wrongly figures, is forty.

"No, just the tea. Excuse me, do you know if Emilio has come here?"

"Emilio who?"

She keeps quiet for a moment. When the waiter asks her the same question as the driver, "Are you okay?", she feels a chill running through her chest, her calves and the back of her head. Blushing, she has no choice but to acknowledge reality: her consciousness is altered, she has no business there, that this Emilio doesn't exist, and she doesn't own a company or make a living as a person but as a kindergarten teacher.

"I have to tell my boss, it's urgent. Help me!"

"What?"

One of the gentlemen throws his cards on the table and leaves the game. He turns his head towards her and is surprised to see her lips and arms trembling.

"What's the matter with you? If you want, I can call the police or the hospital."

From the door, Adriana sees a car with two officers.

"Who are you?" she babbles, still not understanding the situation.

After a verbal tug-of-war they help her remember her name, where she lives, the location of her workplace. She immediately pulls out her cell from her pocket and gets in touch with the daycare center. The director is furious.

"Do you know you've left the kids alone? Do you have any idea what the fuck that means?"

One of the officers gets on the phone and gets to explain what happened. Once the woman has calmed down, Adriana is given the day off. The officers take her to El Grao and refer her to a psychiatrist.

"What you've suffered is a dissociative fugue. It consists of an altered consciousness state and a loss of the sense of identity. It is possible, after a traumatic situation, to undertake a senseless journey, both physically and emotionally speaking, as if you were leaving your own personality.

Finally, it is the doctor who persuades Adriana's boss. Fortunately, she agrees to bring Adriana her cell. When Juan finds out, he is shocked, but Adriana tells him that it is all over. He promises to pick her up when he leaves work in case she gets lost again. The last step is going to the police station, where Roberto is waiting for her.

The interrogation takes place, but it is pretty smooth given the circumstances. When Adriana gets her bearings, she declares that she knows nothing, that she was in the swimming pool, that she has nightmares and constantly relives the episode in the Jacuzzi as if it were happening at that very moment.

As the psychiatrist has explained to her, she will have to learn how to control it.

"Does this picture look familiar? It's from the day of the crime."

It's Juan's Seat León parked by the apartment block. Adriana is surprised, but it fits right in. She wonders if she should ask him for an explanation or not, stunned as she is, until she finally determines:

"He didn't leave our neighbourhood. He knows it's a thirty-minute journey to Oropesa. Maybe he drove there on the sly to keep an eye on me. He is very jealous. But it's unlikely he had anything to do with it." She sees the other image Roberto shows him, the one where she is posing with her friends at the club when she was younger. "I don't think he even knew about the kiss Malory gave me," she adds.

"Pardon?"

"Malory was attracted to me. I know it sounds absurd, but now I'm the one who feels guilty. I told her I didn't want to hurt her feelings, but I had no intention of going on being her friend. I promised her she could always count on me. Please don't say any of this."

"But Malory was a married woman, wasn't she?"

"That's right, but she confessed her feelings to me. Actually, she became as obsessed with me as I am with her now."

"Do you think Brendan might have killed her for that reason?"

"He loved her madly. He never knew, and even if had, I honestly doubt it. He was a gambler, he had a problem, but at no point did I observe him behaving violently.

"And you don't think that maybe he wanted to get some life insurance of hers? Gamblers will do anything to get money." Roberto instinctively reasons.

He touches his mustache. Suddenly a crazy idea crosses his mind: *Juan is an insurance agent. A mere coincidence?* He doesn't think this is the right time to find out.

"It seems to me that, in his case, that makes no sense." Adriana says.

The officer shakes his head and watches her silently, without quite believing it.

"Thanks, you've been really helpful."

At the Oropesa police station, Inspector Almanzor is trying to get information about Alex. The boy may be in his early twenties, but in his shirt and jeans he looks a little older than that. Almanzor sees him pull his shirt down and then clasp his hands together.

"Sit down, please. I need you to explain to me what your mobile was doing in our police vehicle along with some graffiti. I'm all ears."

"Inspector, I swear to you, it wasn't me. I have no idea."

"Why did you change your phone number then?"

The suspect doesn't hesitate.

"I was being threatened by Sinead's cousin and friends. Sinead is Malory's niece."

"Why? So, you knew the victim?"

"Yeah, because I'd been going out with Sinead. Neither Malory nor Eileen accepted our relationship. The girl's friends turned against me too. I didn't do anything to them!" Alex whines.

"If I may ask, what happened between you two?"

The boy bows his head, looking sad.

"Eileen never liked me because I have a three-year-old son. I leave him at the nursery, where Malory worked. Eileen was the one who put all those weird ideas into Sinead's head. Her friends fell for it. I'm very responsible and hardworking. Now that the season is over, and I've given up working as a lifeguard, I'm going to Valencia—near my parents— to look after Ivan and make a living."

"Would you say that Eileen or Sinead had a grudge against Malory? I mean something important enough to poison her."

"I didn't really notice. The only thing is, they argued over a relative's inheritance. Some uncle, I don't know. I'd only been with Sinead a couple of months, so I can't really tell you."

"Where's the boy's mother?" Almanzor asks in an empathetic manner."

"I had no choice but to break up with her. She was on drugs and didn't want to work. I was granted full custody of the kid by Social Services."

The inspector scratches his temple. "Who might have killed the victim?"

As expected, the respondent answers in the negative. At Almanzor's request, he summarizes all the information available. The policeman finds him honest and cooperative in his statement. "Do you have those kids" phone numbers?"

"No, I don't. I only have Sinead's... I hardly have any friends here... apart from her and a barman called Derek. I'm only here to work during the summer... Now because all this scandal, I don't know if they'll open the pool next year."

"Okay, but one more thing. I want you to help me out and let me know anything you know, no matter how insignificant, okay? Even if you leave town."

Alex gets up and shakes Almanzor's calloused hand.

"Count on it, Inspector", Alex promises, showing a deferential attitude.

CHAPTER IX

THE RAIN HAS slackened off a little. Now it's just drizzling, and the community pool has been empty all morning. Perhaps the owners will enjoy it for a few more days, even though the spa and private Jacuzzi are still cordoned off.

On his way to the bar to see his friend Derek, Alex thinks about Sinead. He's enraptured by her beauty and drawn to her curls and freckles. Her clear, deep-set eyes produce a soothing effect on others, as if the whole universe stopped in them. The delicacy of her skin. It seems like an eternity ago that he had the privilege to caress every inch of her body. "Maybe it only amounted to a summer fling," he says to himself. "I don't know, but I also have the right to start anew." He looks both sides, alert, as if trying to protect himself.

As soon as he enters the premises, he summons Derek with a finger. They high five.

"Where are you sitting today, man?

"Right here." Alex points at a table near the wall.

"Here's the menu. Starters are salad and croquettes. For the main course you can choose scrambled eggs or hake."

Alex sits down and reads the words without processing what they mean.

"What? Have you decided yet? You have your head in the clouds." Derek wakes him up.

"Hey, do you know who Sinead's friends are?"

"You're still thinking about that chick?"

"They wanted to beat me up."

"They look familiar, but I don't know any of them. I used to date a friend of hers, Martha, but they fell out. Anyway, I won't let them do anything bad to you."

"Oh! Marta, Yaiza's sister? The one who was in my class at Bachiller in Valencia?"

"Yeah, they used to live there, but they've moved several times."

"OK, man. Well, salad and scrambled eggs."

"And to drink?"

"Orange soda."

"OK. By the way, how long are you staying?"

"Tomorrow morning at 9:00 AM I'm taking the train to Valencia."

Derek returns to the bar to take orders and serve beers. As soon as he can, he sneaks out and brings Alex the tray.

"How long did you say you'd been here?" Alex says, looking at his hands, still not so chapped.

"Three years. You know that with my mother I need money anyway, and here I have an unlimited contract."

"How's it going?"

Just then, another waiter gives him the other dish, shouting: "Scrambled eggs". Derek puts it on the table and goes on:

"After the chemotherapy she's developed pain and ulcers, but it's typical. She's already had several tumours. We had to take her to Houston a couple of years ago, and recently it came back to her, but this time she has been treated in Spain, and it has been easier."

"Do you know anything about your old man?" asks Alex, fearing that he will seem meddlesome.

"We speak from time to time. I told you he owns a circus and travels around to different cities. Here he only comes in summer or in high season, so I won't see him until Easter anyway. He set up a tent in Oropesa because he's friends with the guy from the real estate agency."

"How do they know each other?"

"They studied together at university."

"Hey, do you think people stay long working as lifeguards here?"

"Well, they usually come and do it during the summer. But there are some like Ferran, the one who works with you, who have been around all his life, but the kids change and try different jobs. One of them used to be my friend, but he got kicked out."

"Why?"

"I don't know, he got into trouble with Gerard or one of his employees."

A tall waiter stares at the two young men, snapping his fingers impatiently.

"I have to buckle down," says Derek, "so enjoy your trip. We'll keep in touch."

Alex is squeezing the last bits of food with the fork in his left hand. With the right he goes through the old photos of Sinead on his mobile.

CHAPTER X

BRENDAN MEETS GERARD at the office. Although Helio continues its activity at the apartments of Oropesa, sector 1, these are now much less popular with tourists, due to the media scandal caused by the death of Malory.

Despite being allowed to speak at the office without much interference, Gerard decides to leave Dimas and Marisa, the administrative staff, in charge of dealing with customers who will make complaints about freezers that don't cool and old televisions that stop working. He also tells them to welcome newcomers to the resort.

Gerard closes the white office door so that he can quietly discuss the apartment sale with Brendan. The client takes a chair and sits down in front of the real estate agent.

"Then what's your plan?"

"I want to sell it and with the money I get I may rent one in another area."

"OK, have you thought of any specifics? We have flats about ten kilometres from Oropesa, in Benicàssim.

Brendan can't get rid of the fear of leaving home. Visits from the police forensics and various experts have turned it into a kind of laboratory, from which his memories and the calm that once used to reign, seem to have been removed.

Time weighs so heavily on him that the negotiation seems eternal, ready as he may be to find new accommodation.

"So you're renting this shared penthouse? You'll see how cozy it is. You have a lot of privacy, because it's a low-traffic area, but there are many shops around" Gerard cheerfully assures.

Brendan hears a small closet door squeak. Inside he sees bundles of keys hanging on the wall.

"Gerard, answer me one question."

The other one is stunned because Brendan x-rays him with his eyes.

"Who took your keys?" he finally asks.

"Hey, Brendan. I have no idea. I've already told the police. Maybe they jumped the fence at the pool at night" he scratches the crown of his sparse head. "I haven't touched this key since I made a copy for Lidia, the receptionist. Forensics are still analyzing the crime scene. Looks like no fingerprints have been left."

"But that can't be... OK, Gerard, I'm coming tomorrow to pick up the contract and the keys, right?" he gives up, thinking that, if the agency had something to do with it, sooner or later someone will find out.

The moment of packing, normally very pleasant for the tourists with whom he has lived in the complex, causes him immense pain. He picks up every sweater, trouser and skirt. "What shall I do with them?" He has heard from grief counselors that sometimes you have to get rid of certain objects that can cause an obsession with the deceased, and that only valuable recollections should be kept in mind. *Would it be macabre to give Adriana those clothes?* He wonders. In the end, he decides to carry everything. In the room, hidden among a mountain of papers and pills for erectile dysfunction, appears a black and white portrait of Adriana. It was painted by Malory, with such realism that she could have sold it for a fortune.

He goes through the album from the desktop computer in the living room. He sees himself holding Malory's waist by Samuel Beckett Bridge. "Why, my love." Both of them happy at birthday parties with her parents. Posing on Tara's hill, that mythical place of worship, origin of legends. Finally, he comes across the pictures at the nightclub he sent to the police. He can't hold back his tears.

When he thinks that nothing important is left, except the mobile phone that the investigators have promised to give him back soon, he comes across an agenda where she'd left a password. Instinctively, he enters the email password she didn't bother to delete from the list of recently used accounts.

The first thing he sees is videos of her playing the guitar, an instrument he still has in his room. Then, among so much irrelevant garbage, he comes across a conversation with Adriana, from about six months ago, hidden in the mailbox. To his surprise, he discovers that they were planning a trip to another province to start an educational project together. Malory suggested asking for a loan and putting up money to start the business, to which her friend replied in the affirmative, although without specifying how long they would have to wait.

At no time do they mention their husbands or the many life changes that their plan would entail.

Brendan will no longer be able to verify the firmness of Malory's decision, nor how she planned to act now that they were going to have a child, unless he asks Adriana without Juan knowing. "I can stop by their village to say "hi" tomorrow," he weighs up.

At that moment it occurs to him to say goodbye to Anthony and Daniela, even though he has already spoken to them at the mortuary and at the funeral. Then he will go to see Eileen and Sinead. Anthony is an Uber driver, so Brendan ignores what time may suit him best to meet.

"Hi, Brendan. How are you feeling?"

"Well, Anthony, still very upset. I'm leaving tomorrow. Can I see you for a while?"

"Daniela's got the night shift at the nursing home today. Edith's out with friends. I think I'll finish around eight because I've been with clients all day. You can come after that?"

"Okay, I'll give you a call then. I'll see you later."

"OK, take care."

Not knowing exactly what to do, he decides to walk to the bar area to have a drink and try to forget everything. He asks for a Passport with orange and sits down at the back of the bar, watching the few customers who gather in the place: a fifty-year-old man with a beret who pretends to be an intellectual, a Moroccan couple and a very thin stiff man who is arguing heatedly about football with one of the waiters.

He pays for the drink and asks for change to play the slot machine. Suddenly, the phone rings. He is surprised by a deep, distorted man's voice, with an accent that may be Russian or Ukrainian:

"Get out now. Don't delay!"

"Who are you?" asks Brendan.

"Don't ask, your life is in danger." the man warns him.

There's no one outside, at least not in plain sight. In vain, he looks both ways. On the left he sees only the roundabout presided over by a bizarre modernist monument that leads to a dirt track that the mayor had artificially filled in with earth carried by cranes. On the right he leaves the apartment blocks. His old apartment, number 101, he probably will never see again.

Next, he walks back to his house, still puzzled. In a few seconds he feels the cold metal of a gun pointing at his neck. The hooded man coming from the front blindfolds him.

"Get in the car!" Between the two of them they grab his arm and tie his hands and legs with ropes. The one who speaks gets in the back with him, without taking the gun away from his neck. The other one drives madly through the bumpy waste ground which leads to the beach.

"What are you doing?" It is the only thing Brendan can babble about.

"Shut up or I'll blow your brains out!" warns the man next to him, squeezing the barrel into his mouth. "Now you're going to tell us what you do with whores."

"What? – I've never in my life..."

"Did you kill Lisa?"

"I don't know any Lisa," Brendan answers dryly. The other one punches him in the jaw. His assistant spins and pulls the hand brake.

"Then what the fuck did you do that night you disappeared?"

"I don't know what you're talking about, or who you are."

The guy with the gun kicks him in the testicles. Brendan writhes in pain from the impact.

"I'll ask you for the last time, did you fuck and kill Lisa?"

"No, no, I swear!"

The kidnapper passes the fire hydrant all over his face.

"Be careful!" he screams before opening the door and throwing him into the street like a sack of potatoes. The car slides towards the main roundabout, and then behind the ugly modernist sculpture.

CHAPTER XI

ALMANZOR, WHO IS spending his break playing Pictionary with Sonia and Izan, receives a notification from the switchboard. The operator informs him that a passer-by has rescued Brendan, who is on the verge of a nervous breakdown again.

The inspector shouts," Don't move, I'm coming right away!" He sets off, speeding down the busy ring road which leads to the vacant lot.

Once there, Brendan, without letting go of the old man's arm, tells him that his wallet with papers and money has been stolen.

"Lisa? Did he say her nationality?"

"No, inspector. I don't know her at all. I've never had to go to such places in my life."

"Why else would they bother? Just to steal your money?" Almanzor uses a firm tone.

"You are mistaken, I'm telling you the truth. They're despicable, all for the 50 Euros I had on me."

"Well, let's check if there's a Lisa who's been killed by using a cross-reference database. Keep yourself available if you don't want us to trace your phone. You can get your new ID at Benicàssim. Until then, you'll have a receipt."

Brendan goes away, crestfallen. How many ups and downs is his life going to have?

He decides to ring the doorbell of his Colombian friends' house. They live in 254. He gets to hear Daniela say, "What's the matter, can't I bring my sister?"

Anthony shouts at her and threatens her. She is beside herself.

"I can't stand you," complains Edith, whose voice sounds very close to that of her mother and her stepfather.

"Shall I knock on the door or not? How upset they are. Perhaps my presence will help to calm things down." Brendan contemplates.

Finally, he makes up his mind. Anthony's the one who opens the door.

"Hello, Brendan. Everything OK? You look terrible" the Colombian says, looking up and down.

"Look who's talking," thinks the other, though he doesn't verbalize it. "Why should I proclaim myself the saviour of all couples, precisely me who have lost my own? I won't confess that I've been kidnapped, robbed and assaulted. Let's leave things as they are."

"Anything to drink?" suggests Daniela, standing next to her husband, both still red in the face from the previous tension.

"Yes, a beer, if you have one," replies Brendan, who has sat on the couch with Edith to watch a gossip show in which several celebrities are ripping each other to pieces. After fifteen minutes, already dressed in her sanitary uniform, Daniela kisses Edith on each cheek and then presses her warm, soft lips to Anthony's. "I'm leaving now, I'm going to work. Have a good trip" she says to Brendan before leaving the room. To be polite, the Irishman stays an extra half hour with father and daughter. In spite of the forced talk, one can feel that they don't show a single bit of interest.

CHAPTER XII

THAT SAME DAY, around three o'clock in the afternoon, one of the three mobiles that Gerard has in his semi-detached house has started to ring with one of those penetrating tones that produce headaches.

"Anna, pick up the phone," says the Frenchman, pointing his head towards the room where his wife is laying out her clothes. The cheerful blonde Russian woman, with long blonde hair and wide hips, arrives hurriedly, running barefoot on tiptoe through the room.

"Good evening," she says, and puts the device to her ear. "Excuse me, one question, did you find us on the Internet?" The other one hesitates. The woman is still talking. "Don't worry. I understand it's for tonight?"

"Yes, yes."

"Perfect, then come. Today Valeria, Mia, Roxana are available..."

"And Sofía?"

"No, Sofía's here only on weekends and by appointment...You can find all the photos on our website...It's at 45 Carrer del Montseny street, near the industrial area. When you are in the area call us again and I'll give you the exact address...Thank you".

Gerard's watching one of those American sitcoms where all the roommates work at the same office. He grabs a bottle of Johnnie Walker and pours himself a drink. "Is Daniela already there to greet the clients?" he asks Anna, yawning.

"No, she said she'd be there around nine o'clock. She changed shifts with Ava."

"Are you hungry? Let's have dinner."

The man is about to cook some steaks when suddenly he gets a text message from Lidia.

<"I've got the bills, can you come over?">

He's certain that you don't need to be face to face to sort out an administrative issue, so he senses the girl's going to ask him for a favour, maybe a holiday or a raise. *"She's always sucking up to me to get her way. She must think she's going to become a golden girl as a receptionist."*

<"What do you want?> "he writes.

 <"I need you to come, hurry up.> "

<"Now?">

<"Yes! Please, Gerard.">

<"Are you kidding?">

<"Gerard, seriously, I need your help.">

<"Is there something wrong?">

<"It's urgent. I'll wait for you in the town hall square.">

The promoter drives his BMW to the entrance of the town. He goes slowly, listening to the news on the radio. They're speaking about an ex-commissioner's remaining in prison for the alleged sale of privileged information to set up a network of companies. Gerard finds a free parking space place easily. He walks around, observing the terraces and hotels on both sides, crosses a park and heads for the meeting place.

Lidia is sitting on a bench. She puts her arm around the neck of a girl who is crying and has blood coming out of her lip. When Gerard sees them, he is impressed. Lidia gets up with a jerk.

"Gerard, this is my friend Rocío."

The man carefully examines her hunched back and her dodgy appearance. She's a brunette with extensions, about 5 feet tall, approximately 120 pounds.

"What's happened to you?

"I was... I was hit by the Russian..." Rocío mumbles.

"Vladimir? "He guesses she's talking about his old partner. "Do you know him?"

"Sh-she needs your help, Gerard," Lidia stutters shyly, answering for her.

"What for?"

"Well... could you take her away and give her a job? You know... in the house..."

"So you work for Vladimir?" Gerard is seeking confirmation from the frightened young woman.

"He kicked me out. He told me to go only because I collected a little less yesterday. Look at the punch he gave me" Rocío cries under the lip wound, half-covered by a handkerchief.

"But does he know you were going to talk to me?"

Rocío makes a gesture of denial.

Lidia intervenes again. "No, he doesn't know anything. I told him that you know this man and that he's a b-bastard. She'll be safe with you. But don't get me into trouble, I haven't a thing to do with that world, OK?"

"That son of a bitch is dangerous. I told him not to mix with me anymore," says Gerard. "Do you want a cigarette?"

Rocío politely rejects it. Lidia accepts it, asks for a light and adds:

"Don't let anyone know. She's a lifelong friend of mine. She hasn't reported them out of fear."

"Don't worry. Rocío, if you want, I'll take you there now. This way you'll meet your friends, and you can try working." Gerard offers.

She nods her head. They both say goodbye to Lidia and get in the car.

Alex knocks on the white door of the brothel, which is at street level, eager to see what the new place will bring. Eileen opens and hides behind it, as she usually does. When she sees the young man, she wants the earth to swallow her up.

"You? No! But... what are you doing here?" She says, between indignant and maternal.

"Fuck! That's the same thing I'm thinking about you." Alex takes a step back.

"Don't even think about saying anything, huh?"

"Please don't tell Sinead. I feel so alone, I never..."

"Come in, come in. You wouldn't do this when you were dating my daughter by any chance?" protests Eileen, who calls herself Ava for discretion.

"No, I swear. Admit me."

Eileen bursts out laughing.

"Are you looking for any particular girl?" She says in a sweet tone, yet she can't erase the astonishment from her face.

"The one who picked up the phone gave me several names, but I don't know them."

"Come in, quickly," says Eileen, accompanying him to the room. "How long are you staying?"

"Half an hour, in principle," they look at each other, "and you, you're not available?" he asks resting her upper teeth on her lips and grabbing her, shyly but boldly, by the waist.

"Me? How can you even think of that? No, I'm sorry," says Eileen, without taking his hands away.

"What a pity, I would love to" Although he feels awful, the unexpected situation is getting more and more exciting to Alex.

"No, I don't. Wait here?"

While Eileen is absent, three girls come in turns to greet him reluctantly. When the Irish woman returns, Alex pays her and tells her who he's chosen.

"Oh, Rocío. She's new, she just started. Here, this is your towel," she says.

Then she gently closes the door, leaving the sound of her high-heeled shoes in her wake.

Alex squats in the room, freed from the darkness by a small candle and a coppery light. He still hasn't finished digesting the situation, and wonders if what his ex-girlfriend's mother has told him is true.

"The good thing about this is that neither of us can judge the other morally," he comforts himself in vain.

An instrumental version of Pink Floyd plays faintly on the radio in the back of the room. Five minutes have passed when Rocio appears, covered only by red underwear.

"Hello, how are you? Have you showered yet?" she whispers in a sensual tone to break the ice. The boy stands up and they exchange some topics about the situation, the age, the time she has been in the house and other paraphernalia. Alex enjoys observing the girl's firm, rounded ass. With her back to him, she places the fresh bed linen. His heart begins to race.

However, when he returns to his own flat, puts his son Daniel to bed and finally goes to bed, he has an erotic dream about Eileen. He wakes up startled, guilt-ridden. "It's just an unconscious fantasy," he repeats to himself.

* * * * *

THAT SAME AFTERNOON, Rosa, from Cybercrime, has analysed the record with all the calls that Alex made using his old phone, already disconnected. Perhaps one of them will be useful to clarify his involvement in the case. She prefers to take the initiative and postpone telling Almanzor and Roberto until later. After all, the case is too big for them. She knows that Alex was Sinead's girlfriend, even if it was only for two months. She has discovered that Alex frequented brothels. He has a baby and refuses to give much information about the mother. She thinks he's a deadbeat. *"But who am I to judge, if I'm so lonely?"* she is surprised to think later.

Rosa waits impatiently for Isabel Camacho to appear. She has always thought that Isabel was intelligent, an example to follow, even if her irony sometimes becomes heavy. "It's all because she's very analytical", she justifies her reasoning. That's not a disadvantage. She feels lucky to have met her at the Benicàssim police station. Isabel finally shows up. They shake hands.

"How are you doing, Rosa?"

"I had a lot of work today, analyzing several cases of telephone extortion. I had time to enter all the numbers Alex called on his previous mobile."

"Anything interesting?" Isabel asks with an eyebrow raised.

The search engine threw up codes with the digits I typed in, which weren't even bloody phones. Pictures with Chinese and Russian letters, more pictures of food, strands of fake hair. The calls confirmed what I expected: "the number you have dialled doesn't exist." I went for the next one, this time suspicious, reported several times by other users, specifically as phone spam. When I managed to get through, I was answered by a girl, I'd say in her thirties, with a suggestive voice. She gave me places and prices, without going into much detail. The others are directly whorehouses that advertise on the internet.

"The guy's a little jewel! OK, do you want to go to one?"

Rosa shakes her head.

"There are so many houses, so I don't know which one we should start with. We can geolocate the dodgy addresses. All these calls were made, according to the list given to us by the operator, between May 5th and August 31st. "

"Well, I mean... -Should we interrogate him?"

"I think we should do that when we have something to tell him. We know where he lives now, so... As I was saying, there's a phone belonging to a Yaiza. Apparently, a friend of his."

"And what did she say?"

"She seemed upset. She spoke very highly of Alex. She was nervous, as if she was in love with him. She says he went out with Malory's niece, but they'd split up. She also offered to cooperate with us when she goes to visit him in Valencia."

"I mean, you're saying you came across Russian letters, right? Isabel asks.

"Yes, why?"

"Almanzor has phoned me. He says Brendan was kidnapped. They tied his hands and feet and threatened him. They asked him if he'd slept with a Lisa, apparently a prostitute."

"Can you put that name in the search engine to see if anything come up?"

Rosa does what the boss asks.

"Well, a few results. We'll have to check the photos for fakes."

"OK, have fun. I'm going out to have a cigarette," says Isabel.

CHAPTER XIII

BRENDAN LIES IN bed in room 101. It is his last night in Oropesa and he hopes to get a reasonable number of hours of sleep. Unfortunately, one of his nightmares strikes. This time, Malory emerges from a bloody sea, her eye sockets turned upside down, screaming in an unintelligible dialect. Suddenly she has a normal face again, her sweet face. As if she did not know him, she addresses him in the following terms: "Good evening, sir, you may make a wish." Sure of his answer, Brendan says, "I am forty years old at the moment. I would like to stay this age forever and never be older."

The redhead smiles.

"OK, your wish is my command."

Little by little, her body falls apart and finally turns into a huge pink smoke cloud. The man again shelters himself from his own ghosts between the sheets, those sentinels that guard his dreams; he curls up in the foetal position. Suddenly, he begins to notice his forehead getting colder and colder; a sensation that extends to his eyelids, his mouth, his cheeks, his heart, his belly, his legs.

His whole being becomes paralyzed, and only then does he understand that not having another birthday would mean dying from the most miserable cold, in the most frightening winter that his naive mind could imagine, just as it has happened to Malory.

He wakes up startled and sweaty. He showers with almost boiling water, gets dressed, picks up his contract and the keys that Gerard has prepared for him, and takes the road to his new home. The traffic catches up with him, so it takes him about twenty-five minutes to get to Benicàssim. The navigation system easily takes him to the urbanization.

where two children are crazily playing ball.

Next to the doorway, a boy is waiting. Brendan reckons he must be about twenty-two or twenty-three years old. His name happens to be Manuel. The real estate agent arrives just in time, although a few minutes after they have already started a conversation.

"Good morning. I'm Antoine, from Promociones Helio." He greets each of them with a strong handshake.

At the agency, while they formalize the process, Manuel doesn't stop asking questions.

"Is the beach very far away?"

"No, it's only about ten minutes. You take the first right and then straight on."

"And the shopping centre?"

Antoine spreads out a map on the office table and adjusts his glasses.

"You're here. You have food stores nearby, but the mall... Do you drive?"

"Yes, I do."

The developer takes out a marker and traces the route on the paper.

"So you get on the road, as if you were going to the beach. When you reach this roundabout, take the left exit, and then it's the second or third street. You'll see the signs."

From the surnames on the card, Brendan guesses that Antoine is Gerard's brother, but avoids the comment. Although with much more hair, his prominent forehead and aquiline nose make them very similar.

The man guides them to their new flat, which is located on a ground floor in one of the most discreet buildings. He shows them all the rooms in a way that, according to Brendan, proves that he has a few years of experience in the business.

When the real estate agent leaves, the tenants continue to talk.

"What do you do?" Manuel asks.

Brendan looks at the young man with suspicion.

"I work for an insurance company. And you?"

"Leisure monitor in a children's ball pool. I'm also a football referee on weekends."

"Wow, really? I like football."

"What team do you support?"

"Valencia," he giggles.

"He sounds fake", Manuel thinks. "I thought you'd say some team from your country. Are you Scottish?"

"Irish," Brendan answers indignantly.

"I..... Well, I follow Real Madrid. Actually, I enjoy watching any team. I've also studied Social Education. I'm preparing for a competitive exam to be a state worker."

"Wow, a very busy life."

Brendan steps back to his room. Behind the apparent complicity, there is only protocol. It's all false. Brendan doesn't even think of telling him about his wife's shocking case, something Manuel would have welcomed with disbelief. "He has probably heard about the case on TV without putting a face to the protagonists of the event. I can't trust him. I don't know why, but I've lost my trust   in people and will never get it back."   He starts to Google. "Fatal asphyxiation," "dry ice intake," "dry ice and death," "carbonic snow," "chloroform," "head injury," "head trauma,"   "suicide,"   "depression,"   "marital dissatisfaction,"   "weakness," "loss of appetite," "obsession with loss of a loved one," "gambling." Each term leads to a new one. Sometimes it results in news of senseless deaths or carefully planned murders.   Other times it results from medical encyclopedias: definition, symptoms, treatment, world statistics. It is a hotbed of comments on forums, as ridiculously annoying as his worrying on sleepless nights.

CHAPTER XIV

ADRIANA RETURNS FROM the psychiatrist's office with a piece of paper in her hand.

"What are you bringing?" asks Juan as he gets off his stationary bike.

"She's refused to prescribe some of the pills and told me to take Imipramine."

"So which ones must you stop taking?" he asks as he approaches her.

Adriana gently kisses his lips.

"The hypnotic and the serotonin reuptake inhibitor."

She's been worried for some time that Juan might perceive her as some sort of madwoman.

"Fine, isn't it? Mmm-hmm. You seem to be getting better."

"I don't know, Juan. My boss won't put up with me anymore."

She waits for her husband to refute her claim, but he keeps quiet.

"Do you know what I've thought? That I could set up a school. There are many places to rent in this area. What if I ask for a loan?"

Juan wonders why he had checked out Adriana on that dating app. He sees her as sensitive and dreamy, unlike him, a practical man who travels and meets with businessmen and negotiators.

"But setting up a business is not so easy," he shows off with a condescending air.

"You, you can help me. With all the project and event management you do... I'll sign up for a course, but I need a hand in my first year."

John rests his hand on his chin, skeptical.

"But why are you gonna go into debt like that?"

"I'm just saying, if I get fired, there's not going to be much choice. The jobs that come in the employment pages are crap. I can go on the dole and charge all unemployment benefits together. You'd help me, wouldn't you?

"And quit my job? If it goes wrong, I don't think I'll find a similar one."

"That's not what I mean. Just backing me up on certain issues will do. For other things I can hire a receptionist or call a consultant. Who cares? Everyone has to start from zero," Adriana says.

"I'm not saying you shouldn't, but, if I were you, I'd take some time to think it over. Take advantage of the leave and explain your idea at the town hall."

Adriana nods, pressing her lips to indicate there's another matter to consider. "And why don't we have a child?" she asks with a sad look.

"Of course, darling. There's time for everything. If you focus on a different priority every time, there won't be any problems," Juan assures her. She doesn't know whether to interpret this as a reproach or a simple statement.

On the balcony, Juan is trying to fix a chair with two broken legs. He varnishes it, but the pieces don't stick. Fed up, he loses patience and repeatedly stamps it against the floor until it shatters.

Before dinner he settles into the living room, listening to instrumental music with his headphones on full blast. Sitting at the table, he enters data into a spreadsheet. From time to time, he looks out of the corner of his eye at Adriana, who is still engaged in reading a book. "Anthology of Spanish Short Stories: 1900-1939," the cover says. He is confident now that she has returned to reading, a hobby she had put aside, indicates that perhaps she is really close to overcoming her trauma.

The stability they are achieving in their relationship after so many conflicts, causes him both tenderness and guilt. Concealed among clients and bills, the images flood into his mind. That fateful night, three years ago, they went to the Palm Trees discotheque in Oropesa. He has gone from wanting to control his partner, to conquer happiness, to being dominated by memories and guilt, bloody guilt.

"At that time, Daniela worked behind the bar until six or seven in the morning. That night Adriana, Malory, Brendan and I had had quite a few drinks. The only sober one, Anthony, offered to take Malory and Adriana home in his Uber because they were drunk as hell. He had a back seat full of junk, so we couldn't all fit. Since I had to pick up clients, Brendan and I stayed at the club. What an asshole I was! The wait went on for three hours and when we got back, Anthony couldn't get either of us on our mobile. We had no reception inside. They wouldn't let him in either because he'd forgotten the stamp and the capacity was full. The bouncers got nervous almost immediately, so he gave up.

Anthony stayed with the music on inside the Uber next to the parking lot, smoking cigarette after cigarette for twenty minutes. Brendan hadn't moved from one of the couches in the reserve, where he slept soundly for most of the night."

Juan makes sure Adriana keeps reading and puts his right hand on his head. He remembers his first meeting with Daniela....

Actually, the situation got out of hand. *"Yes, indeed. I was wrong."* He looks at her legs. *"The lipstick looks great on her."*

"What's the matter with you? Cheer up."

"Nothing, I'm just tired."

"Come on, let's dance."

He notices the burning and sweet taste of the shots he's taken. Most people have left, so Daniela comes out of the bar and swings in front of him to the rhythm of bachata. She quickly takes him to that damn room, where she takes off her stilettos and satin dress and keeps on only the red lace bra and the thong. Naked she is even more incredible, and soon he feels her full lips coming down his belly. Before he even notices, she's bouncing on him. He gets her down on all fours and penetrates her hard. They meet again another day, taking advantage of the fact that Daniela has the keys to the club. Juan takes off his jeans and his patterned T-shirt. He has avoided grooming himself so that Adriana doesn't get suspicious and believes his claim that he is going to have a drink with a colleague. He shows up in the room, eager for sex. Daniela plays with the lights and music in the disc jockey's booth. She sits down at the bar, winks at him and beckons him to come closer by waving her index finger. He obeys. The Colombian woman shows him her cell phone.

"Look, I have a present for you."

He gets a tremendous chill when he sees the video on the screen. The moaning that used to excite him now turns out to be creepy. He holds her tightly by the wrists, but she warns him: "Don't move or I'll call Vladimir. If you go too far, he'll shoot you twice." He lets go of her and she slowly goes on talking.

"A girl is coming to help me with the bottles. She works here, but she has no papers. When I tell you, I want you to take the car and drive her home."

"What?"

Daniela demands that he obey and ask no more questions. Lisa is also Colombian, very similar to her, although thinner and with darker skin. She is wearing a camouflage shirt, tight black leggings and a navy-blue vest. She doesn't stop talking and laughing. Juan tries to play along and engage her in conversation. Daniela says she is going to get a bottle and stops at the bottom of the bar. When she returns, she has three shots ready. They make a toast, drink, and continue talking.

After ten minutes, Lisa complains that her mouth is dry. She says she is feeling hot and dizzy. Daniela asks her when she will have customers, and which days she will be free. The answers and the speech become more and more incoherent. When the guest goes to the bathroom to drink water, Daniela explains the real plan to Juan.

"I've poured scopolamine in her drink. I want you to take her to an open field, strip her naked and spread the semen from this pot over her. She won't be aware of it even if she's awake. Then kill her. Inside the backpack you have an axe and gloves."

"What are you talking about? Are you nuts?"

"Do you want to get yourself killed? No, right? Then do what I say!"

"Daniela, what the fuck do you want from me? "

"Do what I'm telling you or they'll pump you full of lead. And don't call the cops or I'll send the video. I'll put it on the internet."

"So that's the game?" Juan thinks. He'll have to find a way to teach her a lesson. He won't give in to her blackmail. When Lisa comes back from the toilet, her cheeks are red, and her eyes are glazed. Daniela beckons to him. Juan doesn't intend to attack Lisa. He'll leave her in her neighbourhood and go away.

Three minutes later, Lisa orders him to stop. She constantly repeats that she is having a client tomorrow, that she is struggling to breathe and that her hands are floating. Before taking her into town, Juan stops on a street in the industrial area, grabs his backpack from under the steering wheel and gets out to pee. He puts the key back in, which takes almost half a minute to turn. Lisa continues to protest.

"Don't you start the car!"

He does exactly the opposite. "What the hell do you want?"

Lisa takes a knife out of her trouser pocket.

"Stop! What are you doing, are you nuts?"

The girl cuts his wrist horizontally. Juan asks her to drop the knife and she obeys as an abductee. He puts the Seat back into gear. After a few seconds, he notices the puncture of the metal on his cheek again. He stops short. He opens the zipper of his backpack slightly. The wooden handle pops out.

"Drop the fucking knife!"

She throws it to the ground under the seat. Juan slips his hands into the latex gloves, then deals her a dry blow with the thick steel blade of the axe. "What am I doing, what am I doing?" He suddenly panics. The blood gushes out of her. Frightened by what he sees, he accelerates, goes past the empty factories praying that the police don't drive by. He takes a deep breath when he reaches the open field. Full of disgust and despair, he strips her naked and pours the liquid in the bottle on her pubis. He looks up to the sky, grabs her by the waist and throws her into the mud. He burns the gloves using a cigarette lighter and leaves. "I'm a murderer," he repeats in his mind as he hears the engine roar.

CHAPTER XV

Daniela WALKS HAND in hand with Edith along the airport terminal. She burns with the desire to put an end to the nightmare. Those who long for the moment to see their loved ones again, turn their heads to the panels. Perhaps the constant change of course lies in our genes. Whether it is true or not, she can't afford to live in hell anymore.

She sees her sister Johana running to hug them both. She carries only her hand luggage.

"Long time no see! How's life?" Daniela says.

"What's up? Edith, you've grown so much!" exclaims Johana, looking closely at her niece, whose body has started changing into a woman's.

Daniela puts on her sunglasses and drives down the highway.

"Do you really think you'll be better off here, Johana?

"I told you, the guerrilla groups are threatening the government. Many women have been killed in the communes. And Dad... well, you got rid of him, but he's still got a temper. He's always annoying all of us."

"But here it's a nuisance. Anthony's not the nicest guy in the world," Daniela explains as she takes the detour to Oropesa and stares at Edith slyly, with the invisibility afforded by her black glasses.

The girl nods her head in the back seat. Johana looks her sister up and down.

"You're seriously asking me to go back to that hellhole? I never would.

"We don't have to go back to Colombia! With the documentation I'm going to give you, you'll have papers to be allowed to move anywhere in Spain. You just have to trust me" Daniela assures while she turns on the radio.

"False documentation? Won't we be caught?" her sister asks in despair.

"Look, Johana. In Medellín I used to work as a waitress, cleaner, geriatrician. Everything I have I've earned: my studies, English... The man who was to be my husband thought he was tougher than the bottle, and he must have died or ended in Alcoholics Anonymous. My roommate, Paola Andrea, she really taught me how to be free. Freedom should not be given up," she concludes, slowing down to enter the urban center.

"But where do you plan to go?"

"Let me think about it. Far away, to Madrid, to Barcelona, it doesn't matter. Well, here we are."

She parks the Seat Cordoba next to the Helio Promotions agency, where Gerard and his partner Marisa are dealing with some tourists. As soon as he finishes with the first client, the French man gets up to greet them.

"Good afternoon, Daniela. Hello, Edith. What's your name? I'm Gerard, nice to meet you."

"Good afternoon, my name's Samantha," lies Johana.

"Come in and sit down."

Looking at the newcomer, Gerard begins to explain the steps to follow.

"Well, as your sister must have told you, we have apartments for rent without any commitment to stay. Since you have just come and don't have a salary, the best thing is to count on Daniela as a guarantor. The only thing I will need is your documentation: passport or national identity card."

"Is a deposit required?" Johanna/Samantha asks with some concern.

"Calm down, I'll lend it to you" Daniela intervenes.

Gerard buttons his shirt all the way up.

"Yes, I need a two-month advance. As you know, apartment 101 has a price reduction. No problem, but given that Daniela's friends lived in it, many people who are superstitious don't want to rent it. It's already furnished. Actually, the accident happened in the hot tub that we've already closed. They've opened an inquiry and..."

"Take it easy, Gerard. I've already explained it to her. Well, he's got to show you the flat, so we're off. Anthony's waiting. Will you come round when you've finished? "interrupts Daniela.

"Of course, I'll see you later."

* * * * *

THE DAYS GO by and Johana still hasn't found a job. She's handed in some resumes for waitressing positions. Daniela has asked Gerard to use his contacts to help her sister, to which he has responded "You know I do what I can, but I am not God."

Daniela thinks she must make an effort to call her Samantha, even though her real name is Johana. Anthony doesn't know anything, because when they met in Medellín she only told him that she had four sisters and one brother. *"Everything is going to be fine,"* she often repeats herself.

"What the fuck, that's my life: washing what I don't like about myself and turning a blind eye." She prepares once again the geriatric assistant's suit. She feels strange. She doesn't lie about going to the nursing home this time, where she works every day from Monday to Thursday, even though she runs the brothel on the weekends. She's only had to make it with those men sometimes, when Gerard and Anna ask her to. Everything is possible by camouflaging her under a second part-time contract as a cleaner.

She lives surrounded by half-truths, declaring only part of her income. *"All the decisions I've made have been in my own legitimate defense. I don't have much left of the money I collected for the life insurance, because Anthony didn't resign himself to respecting my property."* She must fly like a dove. She has to listen to the advice that Paola Andrea gave her.

At the nursing home, she reviews the daily records of every patient with her colleagues. She checks if they have urinated and defecated, if they had dinner the night before, if they are eating well. Dressed in her white suit and blue gloves, she starts changing diapers. Then she meets with her group and starts giving breakfast to the elderly. She pays special attention to one man affected by Alzheimer's. Milk with cookies and cereal, all crushed. She cleans him with the bib. The man smiles and she caresses the beautiful white hair on the back of his neck.

When she returns home, she is overwhelmed by her own good mood. What if he stays a little longer to see if their relationship is mended?

The living room door has slammed shut. So as not to lose good manners, she locks the entrance door before going in. She turns the doorknob to the left and, when she pushes it, her brain projects the strange image it has received through the glass.

Anthony, with his back to her, stands in the center of the room. His butt in the air, pants and belt unbuttoned below his knees. Covered by the stocky torso is Edith, whose lips and legs are trembling. She is naked, covering her breasts with her hands. It all goes by very quickly. Daniela shakes Anthony by the arms.

"You pervert!" How dare you, you son of a bitch?"

"But it was her, she's crazy..." Anthony stammers as he turns around.

"He's lying!" the girl screams.

The mother stares at him for a few seconds. She slaps him on the right cheek. With hardly any time to react, Daniela gets punched sharply in the eye. She remains motionless, sprawled out on the floor.

Edith looks at the objects on the table. With both hands she grabs Daniela's sewing machine, which is next to the math book. Without thinking, she runs to

Anthony, who hasn't turned around completely, and hits him on the temple with uncontrolled force. She emits a high-pitched scream as he watches him fall to the side, on top of her mother, who, despite having her eyes open, still doesn't seem to have fully recovered her consciousness. Blood squirts out of the man's face and runs down the floor.

When she reaches full perception of the gravity of her action, Edith, still naked, can't help but scream:

"He's dead!"

Daniela gets up and runs towards her to cover her mouth with one hand.

"Hush, hush, it was me," she whispers.

"No, Mom! No! What happened?" Edith whispers, resisting to verbalize her feelings. A stream of thoughts crosses her mind. She puts on her pajamas. "I've killed a person," she repeats in her head. "Only God can take life. And I've taken it from him, but I would do it again. I'd hit him again, protecting the one I love. He's not my father. He never loved me."

Daniela feels the weight of her own body fall on the mop that she uses to clean the blood. Meanwhile, a neighbour has called the local police station. After a few minutes, they pound on the door insistently. "Police!" says a voice from the landing.

Daniela comes upon Almanzor, who, with a face almost as white as hers, is about to put handcuffs on her.

CHAPTER XVI

A CIRCUMSPECT EMPLOYEE tells Almanzor and Roberto that their turn has come. The agents don't have the IMEI from Alex's old phone, so the search takes a few minutes.

"It belongs to Alejandro Figueroa Salas. We've already provided a report to an agent from your brigade."

"I'm the head of the investigation. All we need is a call log for the last three months of use."

Back in the office with the document, Almanzor dictates the numbers to Roberto, holding the two stapled sheets firmly in his hands. A first female voice announces to the officer the rates and services until Roberto hangs up.

He gets a similar response again up to three times; it goes to voicemail on others.

"He seems to have gone to massage parlours for a while, stopped when he met Sinead, and returned after leaving her," Robert suggests.

"This cell number," says Almanzor, pointing repeatedly at it with his index finger.

"What about it?"

"Several girls advertised with it. The photos seem to have been taken in the house itself. They must have changed several times. A deactivated advertisement, from about three years ago. I recognize those lights and the dance floor. It's Palm Trees Nightclub."

"So did Alex use to go there?"

"No, Roberto, the place changed hands. Gerard was the proxy until he got tired and preferred not to get into trouble. Do you remember the South American woman who was raped and murdered?

"Yeah, the one who showed up in the wasteland."

"Open that folder. Zoom in. See? There in the background. The day Daniela, Malory, Adriana, Juan and Brendan all went to the disco. She was probably a prostitute in Palm Trees. Daniela knew her and for some reason she hid it. Excuse me, I have to call Rosa."

Almanzor puts the earpiece in his ear. After two rings, he hears the beep.

"Almanzor, any progress?"

"Good morning, Rosa. Hey, can you check a number for me? Alex called and it's not on the list you gave us."

The other cop is silent for a few seconds.

"I don't understand. You've been looking at the records on your own?" she asks, irritated.

"But it's the same thing you did, you and Isabel. "Almanzor gets it off his chest, even though he knows he's risking his job by mentioning the commissioner.

"I have already given you last month's list."

He provides her with the number, without getting anything in return.

"Anyways, the case... the documentation of Samantha that the Civil Guard gave me was false. According to Interpol, her name is Johana Vélez Arango.The surnames remain unchanged, but the name has been changed. She and Daniela are real sisters. She probably brought her to Spain by giving her papers. We need to know how she did it.

"Come on, give me all the details and we'll check it out."

Almanzor hangs up. He's got a hunch.

"Let's get into Daniela's e-mail. I need you to stay here and analyze all the messages. Call me back at the earliest."

"But, Almanzor, are we really interested in investigating a crime that's already been solved? The murderer is in jail" Roberto explains. "She was found dead, mutilated with an axe. What does it matter if she was a regular at that place? We have to find out what happened to Malory."

Almanzor keeps listening to him, but not looking at him. On the screen, is a news story and an identification log.

"Correct, but what did the Russians say to Brendan? They accused him of sleeping with a certain Lisa and killing her. Look here, Roberto. It's the same woman, the one from the club. You know what I think? Daniela made up a sister and said she was the one who'd died so she could collect an insurance policy. Brendan works in a brokerage!"

"And they didn't notice?"

"Roberto, do you know how many forced disappearances there are in Colombia? Thousands! It's a state crime. They wipe them off the map and exploit them here. It doesn't matter if the Civil Guard searches international databases, there's no trace. They never revealed her full name or identified her."

"So Daniela forced the man to rape and kill her. And the Irish guy is involved?

"In Lisa's or his own wife's case, we don't know. The Russians are extorting money. There are some very nasty people around here. I'm going to visit Alex and then Brendan to settle any doubts.

Almanzor returns home for lunch. After a while, Sonia comes back with their son, Izan, from school, and the three of them cook lentils with chorizo.

After coffee, the inspector watches a stage of the cycling Tour of Spain, which he finds as exhausting as police work.

"I've got stuff to do this afternoon." He announces, getting up to leave and return to work.

"When are you coming home??" Sonia asks him, upset as she watches Izan calculate a sum.

"Tonight. Now I'm going to interrogate two people," says Almanzor, hurrying to get his folder.

Sonia frowns and nods her head.

"Have you seen this piece of news? "Oropesa: Kidnappers of deceased Irish woman's husband are wanted."

"Seems like there are a lot of patrols going on at once. They'll let me know."

Almanzor says goodbye to Sonia and Izan with kisses and rushes to the car park. He feels that he is unable to handle everything. His mind needs to solve the riddle, but he must work out his steps well. "If I had the gift of ubiquity, life would treat me better," he thinks as he smiles to himself.

He knows that Brendan has moved to Benicàssim, so he decides to show up unexpectedly to surprise him. The door is open, so he enters without knocking. It is a block of flats with a swimming pool, in a quiet area managed by Dulcemar, the local branch of Helio Promotions.

In his usual deliberate temperament, he slowly climbs the stairs to the first floor, looks for the right flat and finally rings the bell. Much to his surprise, he finds Sinead answers the door. She stares at him in equal astonishment, pushing a lock of her long red hair back from her face. She is wearing blue tracksuit pants and plush sandals. She looks sleepy.

"Good morning."

The inspector stands firm and sticks out his chest.

"Good morning, Sinead. What are you doing here?"

"I've come to spend a few days with my uncle. Is everything all right?" she asks with concern.

"Can I speak to Brendan?"

"What for?"

"I need to ask him a few questions."

Sinead remembers the policeman's kindness during the wake and opens the door for him.

"Okay, come in."

Manuel, sitting at the table in the dining room, raises his head from his notes on the Social Education competitive exam he is working on. He is surprised to see the inspector, but when Brendan greets him with familiarity, Manuel understands that the two men know each other. The student watches in surprise from the table without understanding what is going on. Sinead walks away to her room, fiddling with her mobile phone.

The arguments with Eileen were already unbearable, so when Sinead asked for permission to go to Brendan's house for a few days, her mother did not put up much of a fight.

"Brendan, I need you to confirm a couple of things for me." Almanzor tells him.

"Are you going to take my statement? Unfortunately, I don't know any more than I told you."

"No, no, we can only do that at the police station. I just want to get a few facts."

"Okay, tell me."

"Do you recognize this girl?" He shows Brendan a photograph.

"Not really."

"She's Johana, Daniela's sister, but she claims to be called Samantha."

Brendan repeatedly shakes his head, looks down and then raises his head again. His hands are shaking.

"Does this one look familiar?"

"No, I'm not sure... Now that you mention it, I think it's that girl who was killed, right? It was in all the papers."

"Yes, her name's Lisa. I suppose you know that Daniela murdered her husband, right?"

The Irishman nods.

"Have you heard that Anthony used to abuse Daniela?"

"No, I can't really say, but I never liked those Colombians. We used to hang out with them only when Malory felt like it. Anthony was an antisocial who was always getting into fights. The day I was kidnapped..."

Manuel lifts his head from his notes, cranes his neck in their direction, his eyes wide.

"Wait a minute! What's all this?" He asks, astonished.

"I don't like to remember, Manuel. That's why I didn't tell you."

"What the hell are you talking about? You've been lying to me!

Who the hell are you?"

"Don't interrupt, let him finish," Almanzor orders with an authoritative tone.

"Manuel, listen. I'm Malory's husband, the woman who was killed in Oropesa. I'll explain later, I haven't a thing to hide." Brendan defends himself.

To Manuel, the assertion conveys precisely the opposite. A lot of scenes he's seen in documentaries about serial killers, go through his mind in which the least expected, ends up killing those closest to him.

Almanzor insists, "Go on."

"The day the Russians beat me up, I went upstairs to say goodbye to Anthony and Daniela. I heard them screaming. They were arguing because one of her sisters was coming and Anthony didn't approve of it."

"We believe that Daniela is in the business of forging documents and making money from it. We're also aware that sexual services were being peddled.

at Palm Trees Nightclub. Did you know?"

"Not at all, Inspector."

Manuel and Brendan stare at each other in hostility.

"Where were you on the night of August 20, 2015?"

"Hey, what's this? You said it wasn't an interrogation." protests Brendan, increasingly perplexed.

-Don't worry, we're just trying to find out if you witnessed any scenes that might help us."

"Well, I have no idea, I stayed home, I guess."

"I'll refresh your memory. You went to Palm Trees."

"Maybe, we went there in the summer with Juan and Adriana." Brendan answers reluctantly.

"Did you see any of those women?"

"No, I didn't. I told you. Nothing's gonna bring Malory back! What the hell are you doing to find the killer? You aren't doing anything!"

"Brendan, that's not true" the cop says patronizingly. "We know you work as an insurance agent. Check if anyone with the surnames Vélez Arango has contacted your agency.

Still looking sideways at the cop, Brendan gets up and grabs the laptop on the table near Manuel, who's now examining him with a grimace of anguish, his hands on his belly. After a few minutes of searching the database, the information is displayed on the screen. "Lisa Velez Arango. Policy made in June 2014".

"Suspicions are confirmed. Identity theft. Daniela may have disguised herself or used someone else. I should also point out that the nightclub was owned by Gerard, so perhaps one of those two was involved in Malory's murder."

Brendan makes a fist and takes a deep breath. "But Lisa's rapist... Is he out of jail?"

"No, it couldn't have been him, as he's still serving his sentence. We'll keep talking. I have work to do," concludes Almanzor, shaking both men's hands and heading for the door.

When the policeman leaves, Manuel hesitates between shutting up or scolding his roommate. "Hey, Brendan, this is crazy. I don't want to live here anymore," he says, standing up and waving his hands.

"Manuel, I need you to stay. You've studied violent behaviour, you know a bit more than me, don't you?"

The young man shrugs while Brendan informs him. With her ear to her bedroom door, Sinead listens to what they are talking about; the holiday with Adriana, the Jacuzzi, Lidia, the maintenance company, the lifeguards. She comes closer when she hears the name of her ex-boyfriend, Alex. She consumed by doubts, wondering whether her uncle is hiding something and is purposefully remaining evasive.

"Don't worry, she's a big girl. She's not going to be scared because we talk about these things," Brendan tells Manuel, while looking at Sinead out of the corner of his eye.

Jorge Sánchez López

CHAPTER XVII

September 8th

SPECIAL PROCESSION TIME in Valencia. Following the beat of the drums, children parade around, dressed in turbans, blouses and baggy pants. Women wear mantillas, while men look like warriors. Almanzor makes his way through the crowd, which forms a semicircle to admire the singularity of the parade, until he finds the point where he is meeting up with Alex. The young man is standing, separated from the group. He is carrying the baby in one hand and a bag in the other. Despite his slight smile, the inspector finds his face indecipherable.

"How small he is. How old is he?"

"Eight months." Alex answers proudly.

"What's his name?"

"Ivan."

The inspector mentions the similarity of the name with that of his son Izan, who started crawling at that age. He adds:

"What are you carrying in that bag? I'll hold it for you.

"This? Baby clothes. A friend gave them to me because they no longer suit his son. Yaiza, my girlfriend, is working, so I picked up the clothes before talking to you."

He remembers Judith, the mother, with her little wiry face, matching her eyes, smoking and snorting cocaine on the terrace, wrapped in her flannel pyjamas. In the flat, Alex rocks the baby in his crib. Lying on the sofa, Almanzor is determined to make conversation with him before getting straight to the point.

"I'm glad, you've got your life back on track."

"New sensations are coming," he thinks as Sinead takes the tiny Ivan in her arms. She may have been the ultimate girl, but he can think of powerful reasons why he has ended up with Yaiza. Malory tells him about the boy's physical and psychological development when he collects him from the nursery. She argues with her sister about which of the two will do Alex the favour of looking after Ivan so that he can go on an errand. The doctor informs him: "the drug produces toxic effects on hepatic metabolism and digestive capacity."

"Yeah, we've only been together for a few days. We already knew each other, he studied with me. We've rented an apartment here." He says to Almanzor.

"Alex, we mustn't get distracted, so I need you to be honest. Do you like prostitutes?"

"Cut the lecture, will you?"

"Last summer you made a lot of missed calls that give you away, and in other cases you have one to two-minute conversations."

Alex blushes and then looks for the cop's complicity.

"I don't know... I just got dumped by my girlfriend and as a man I have my needs" he admits.

Almanzor's expression doesn't change.

"Can you give me the names, describe them, or tell me where they work?

The young man remembers a myriad of scenes of passion, which seem to him, to have happened an eternity ago.

"I have no idea. I don't remember anymore."

"Are you trying to obstruct the police investigation?" the inspector accuses him.

"Not at all" the young man declares, disgruntled.

"The thing is, they left your name and phone number under the windscreen wiper on our car at Malory's funeral, along with the graffiti. I don't care if you have an orgy or smoke a thousand joints, but we know that Anthony called you up shortly before he died at Daniela's hands. You talked to him for two minutes the first time, but you didn't answer the second." Almanzor says slowly.

"Go tell it to the marines."

"Don't make me lose my patience. That woman has been a victim of murder unless proven otherwise. This is how good forensics reason. Your number's there and you've changed your phone. A bit suspicious, don't you think?"

Alex scratches his nose and chin. "I told you the truth. I was threatened by Sinead's friends. Besides, Anthony also told me he'd kill me if I accused him. I was the lifeguard... a lot of people said it had been me, or thought I knew who'd done it, but I'm innocent."

"And why would Anthony accuse you of something like that?"

"He was nuts, he was always yelling at his wife... I was used to them at the pool, a lot of times. He'd also hang out with bad people and get into brawls in the neighbourhood."

"Why?"

"I have no idea... Sometimes Spaniards and Russians would come with strange cars, he'd get in, argue with them... I think they were dealing drugs. They wouldn't even leave the estate."

Almanzor pauses and looks at the screen of his Samsung. "Does this number ring a bell? You called six times."

"No, I don't know" Alex replies, irritated.

"My colleagues have gone to Doctor Fleming Street, but there's nobody there. It's a doorway at street level, with the blind always down. Have they moved?"

Alex tries hard to conceal a mischievous smile. "They must have gone to San Antonio Street."

"You've been there?"

"Yes, two months ago." He lies about the time elapsed, so as not to give an even greater impression of promiscuity.

"With what girl?"

"Rocío, Spanish, brunette, nice tits. What does it matter? Listen, I just want to start from scratch, forget about everything... I'm studying, and my life has changed completely. Don't say anything to my girlfriend or incriminate me."

"I'm afraid we can't totally rule out your involvement in the crime."

As if he'd followed the dialogue, the baby breaks into tears. Alex runs to comfort him. He excuses himself to go to the kitchen for a moment and, when he returns, he starts peeling and cutting a pear for the little boy.

"You can't accuse me," he protests childishly, almost crying.

"If you don't give us a reason for it," the inspector corrects him, patting him on the shoulder. "Finally, you were working for Gerard. What might he have to do with the crime?"

"I was only there in the summer. Started in May, just before the tourist season. Gerard seemed to be a nice guy. He was into luxury, but he wasn't mean or violent."

"All right, thanks for your cooperation." Almanzor steps on the gas as he reflects upon the stage of life he's at.

Without realizing it, he has shifted from training future criminologists and covering cases of robbery, kidnapping and disappearances, often with successful results, to chasing the shadow of a "crime" that may just be a suicide or an accident. Both hypotheses keep forensic experts at odds, and he is only looking for people who knew the alleged victim, to go after suspects, even if the killer could be a Colombian man who has already died. He will soon resume his academic activity and request a transfer or prepare for another specialty.

When he gets home, he spends the rest of the afternoon reading a story to Izan and talking to Sonia. He eats a sandwich and a piece of fruit for dinner. At last, he lies down next to her, hugs her, closes his eyes and thinks about a police promotion that may also be a pipe dream.

CHAPTER XVIII

ALMANZOR'S SLEEP HASN'T been restful enough, and as soon as the alarm goes off at seven o'clock, he wakes up with reddened eyes. He checks he has a missed call from Roberto. What did he want at four in the morning? Before having breakfast, he tries to find out.

"What's up, Almanor?"

"What's new?"

"You're gonna freak out when I tell you. I found a video..."

Unexpectedly, Sonia shouts at him: "Come on, man! What are you up to? Izan is already dressed, and we are late!" They keep arguing in the Ford Mondeo. She drives all the way to the police station, never ceasing to reproach him for only existing for the job.

"Well, Izan, give me a kiss. Be good in class" When he says goodbye, Sonia resumes driving, on her way to the boy's school and then to the institute where she works.

Roberto is waiting at the office, with one leg forward and his arms stretched out.

"Who appears in the video?"

"Juan and her. She sent it to him by e-mail.

They slept together in room at the nightclub. They had turned it into a hotel. We have to analyze it. The date matches Lisa's death."

"What does it say in the message?"

"Here you go," in red letters. A warning. It doesn't specify the subject.

The slight background noise of the recording is annoying and the image slightly blurred, but you can see the bodies moving, a chest of drawers, a broken mirror on the left and red curtains in the background.

"Is that all?"

"No, Jose, wait. I'm going to enlarge it. What do you see there?"

Almanzor tries hard to visually discriminate the details.

"That in the half-open drawer... The edge of an axe!"

"Exactly, the same weapon that was used in Lisa's murder. That thing on the bedside table is a pack of gloves."

"Juan killed her! The old man's semen that was put on the body had to be pushed into the bottle by Daniela."

"The man denied knowing Lisa and didn't even mention Daniela. They caught him anyway because the existence of that den was an open secret," Roberto remembers.

"He must have slept with both of them. Daniela saved the semen when she washed herself and blackmailed Juan into spreading it over Lisa's body.

"Of course. Then she pretended that Lisa was her sister, made that statement at the insurance company and collected the compensation. Lisa was an undocumented immigrant, as if she didn't exist. They bought the lie."

"It makes perfect sense. Let's go to Benicàssim!"

The agents get in the car and set off. Suddenly, the repeater rings. It's the local police.

"This is Z-42. Go ahead, dispatch."

"We have a 10-37 code."

"Received."

"Two Russian men, at the station. Possession of cocaine, 2 grams. False documentation. Stolen Mazda 3 Skyactive Evolution with license plate 8253 Delta-Zulu-Victor."

"Criminal record?"

"Yes, they're known in the area. Shoplifting and assaulting women."

Almanzor thanks the operator and hangs up.

"They've been arrested. Can they be the same ones who kidnapped Brendan?" asks Roberto.

"Surely, but since they were hooded, we don't know either. They are many. I think they didn't know who was with Daniela, if it was Brendan or Juan, so they attacked the first one they caught."

"This Vladimir had to testify when they killed Lisa."

"Yes, he denied everything. He said he didn't exploit girls, but he was fined 2000 Euros."

* * * * *

THE NEIGHBOURHOOD WHERE Juan and Adriana live is perfect for families with children. Many schools nearby, spacious houses with blue roofs, parks and all kinds of shops around. The couple, standing in the middle of the sidewalk, talk to a boy and a girl.

Through the open window, from the other end of the wide avenue, Almanzor and Roberto deduce that it is Lidia, the receptionist at the hotel in Oropesa, and a boy they can barely make out.

"Have you seen this? What motherfuckers. They've punctured my tyres and spray-painted me. "For Anthony"," says Juan.

"Holy shit, man! How come?!" exclaims Fran, the employee of Gris.

"Well, I have no idea. I had nothing to do with it. I only found out from the newspaper that Daniela killed him."

Fran puts her hands to her forehead.

"Why?"

"She used to put up with abusive behaviour. Then they had a fight and she killed him."

"You leave me dumbfounded... Well, just report it and they'll be arrested."

"Aren't you working today, Ad-driana?" Lidia stammers.

The agents approach quickly, still unnoticed.

"No, I'm still on leave. I'm going to the doctor this week to see if I can be discharged. "Lidia slightly taps on Juan's leg. "I'm off today."

"Then what will you need?" Fran asks Juan.

"What I told you. For the town disco, a mixer, theatrical smoke and fog and a technician to install the lights."

Fran opens the trunk and points out:

"Look, I brought the table. It's a model..."

Suddenly, Adriana turns her head towards the police car, from which she sees Almanzor and Roberto get out, diverting the group's attention.

"Good morning, identify yourselves." The inspector, with arms akimbo, directs his body towards Juan.

"Is there a problem, Officer?"

"Juan Fernández, you are under arrest for the death of Lisa Vélez..." announces Almanzor, throwing him against the hood of the car and handcuffing him.

While the detainee is escorted to the back seat, Adriana suffers another nervous breakdown. "Shit! Why?! What the hell is going on?!" She falls to her knees, crying and lets her arms fall to the ground. Her face turns into a pale, unhinged grimace. Lidia and Fran pick her up from the ground without her putting up any resistance, and between the two of them they hold her up.

Roberto waits for her to stop wobbling and adds:

"We have proof that your husband killed a woman at Palm Trees Nightclub three years ago, at a party which you also went to."

"That's impossible!" Adriana screams.

Roberto calls another patrol car, while his friends try to calm her down. Within two minutes, they arrive. Eventually, one of the agents accompanies Almanzor and the detainee, who rolls inside the vehicle, to take him into custody and put him on trial. Meanwhile, the rest of the police officers take Adriana, Lidia and Fran away. In private, Roberto tells Adriana what they have found out and conveys his suspicions to her.

"We have evidence that he acted under coercion."

"But who threatened him?"

"Believe it or not, it was Daniela. I'm sorry to say she slept with your husband and extorted him to kill Lisa. I'm sorry to say she slept with your husband and extorted him to kill Lisa. I don't know if the threat could be an extenuating circumstance. We don't do the sentencing."

As empathetic as Roberto is, Adriana's already stopped paying attention to the details. Now she feels that she doesn't know who she is. Her whole life seems to her like a lie or a bad dream from which she wants to wake up. The present cuts her throat and it is impossible for her not to sink into the mud of the past.

She hides under the sheets in broad daylight. When she stretches out her legs, she has the feeling that she is surrounded by music like that of the circus next to Malory's house. She witnesses her body falling off a cliff. The tired melody turns into white noise and then into the soundtrack of a horror movie.

A man wearing black snow gloves appears and gives Malory a daiquiri with frosted ice. She is inside the hot tub and looks puzzled, but she accepts the offer. She starts drinking and gags on some ice. Her body sinks. The water turns red. The foam is triggered and produces a pleasant whisper, similar to that of the sea.

On the right, Adriana perceives another upright female figure, whose hands and face are made of wax and melt. After that, the abdomen does the same. The deforming lump remains attached to the ground. When she regains consciousness, she thinks that she must have gone mad, or perhaps she is sane enough to get out of the stupid naiveté she has been in since birth.

CHAPTER XIX

WHEN SHE HAS finished making arrangements with the bank, Eileen returns home and reads once again, with great satisfaction, the words of the will, which she knows almost by heart:

I, Amy Ferguson Markey, hereby appoint as heirs in equal shares my sister, Deidre Ferguson Markey, and her daughters, Malory O'Dálaigh Ferguson and Eileen O'Dálaigh Ferguson, the former being substituted by her spouse, Ryan Malloy Sheedy, and the latter two being substituted by their respective spouses, Mr. Brendan Sean O'Domhnaill and Mr. Héctor Mendoza Martínez.

Her eyes are blurry. It's her first boat ride with her Hector. She's on vacation in Spain with her family. She spends the afternoon with that handsome, tanned boy. They exchange phone numbers. They talk online for hours. She goes back to Valencia. They celebrate their wedding and choose Venice and Croatia for their honeymoon. Sinead, three kilos at birth. Eileen hears on the news that Hector has just crashed into the rocks. She faints.

Apparently, since her aunt is not aware of the changes, she hasn't made any changes to the legacy. No longer will Eileen have to be content with working as a part-time gym cleaner, and complementing it with the task of opening the door to all those perverts.

In the closet she keeps the beautiful silk dress that the nuns of the parish gave to Malory, and which now belongs to her. She hasn't tried it on since Brendan left Gerard in charge of giving her the clothes.

Her image in the mirror shocks her, as she looks taller and thinner than usual. Despite surpassing her sister in height, she comes off worse in physical comparison to Malory at twenty-three, on the latter's graduation day. Malory never wore it again, so Eileen feels it has been an eternity. She remembers with sadness that party and dinner with her sister and her parents.

The double loss she has suffered makes her rethink whether she will be happy staying in Spain or not. "I'm moving to a villa, even if it's in this very area. 300,000 Euros will do me good. I'll throw a party, invite the people from the neighbourhood and put on my dress so that everyone can see it," she says to herself with great satisfaction...

An evening alone with Malory in Dublin. Her mother is at the supermarket and her father is travelling to Geneva for a biology conference. Eileen is twelve years old when Malory, nearly nine, cuts her own hair with a pair of scissors and, as soon as her mischief is over, rushes to confess it to her. Malory gets a good scolding, although the matter is settled as soon as they go to her aunt's hair salon. Malory plays the piano for a school exhibition and gets a standing ovation. The little girl reaches thirteen. They talk about the boys they flirt with and Eileen gives her advice...

The doorbell rings. As expected, Brendan returns with Sinead in the car around twelve in the morning. It's Monday and the girl is not starting school until

Wednesday, so she has enjoyed a few days with her uncle, who is working the afternoon shift at the company this week.

"Hello! Did you have fun?" says Eileen behind the door.

"Haven't you heard about this?" Brendan replies, showing his sister-in-law the paper.

"Man Arrested For Poisoning And Killing Colombian Woman In Oropesa," the headline runs. Eileen reads the whole article carefully and squeezes the paper between her fingers.

"Juan? How is that possible? Son of a bitch! You see, and Malory hanging out with that scumbag!" she screams when she finishes processing the news.

Several tears roll down Sinead's cheeks.

"Mom, do you think he's the one who killed Aunt Malory?"

"I hope not, because, if I come across him, he's going to get his ass kicked."

Brendan's got his finger on her shoulder.

"Look, the guy I live with is a social educator. We've found out which youth centre Edith is in. Edith, Daniela's daughter. As my flat mate passed the exam, she was sent there due to its proximity. I have begged him to keep an eye out and to pressure them to get information out of the girl. I also called Adriana, but she has had a mental breakdown and still won't accept what her husband has done," says Brendan.

Eileen pays no attention to him, because she is still confused and is only capable of expressing anger.

"All those pigs are murderers, fighters and drug addicts. If she'd listened to me, they wouldn't have destroyed her."

Brendan intuits a sense of loathing towards him, implicit in his sister-in-law's words, but then she pauses and tries to calm down.

"Do you want a drink?"

The woman comes back with a tray full of cured meats and two large bottles of soda. While Eileen continues to communicate her ideas of revenge, Brendan reflects on how to find out the identity of the murderer, a challenge that has threatened to undermine his health for weeks. He prefers to get out of there in a hurry rather than become the target of criticism. "Adriana was Malory's best friend, but the blame for Juan being a murderer lies solely with him." he thinks, although he doesn't dare to express it aloud.

"Well, I have to go, girls," he sees them off, hugging and giving two kisses each.

He rushes off so as to have time to eat and prepare for the workday. Meanwhile, Manuel nervously goes to the child protection centre, on his first day as an interim educator, replacing a person on maternity leave. The director, José Ramón, a strong man in his fifties, with dark, side-parted hair, explains to him how the residence works, the protocols that are followed and the evaluation, intervention and reporting procedures carried out.

Among the files he reads are cases of gender violence and child abuse, drug abuse on the part of parents, serious illness, educational negligence, lack of schooling and lack of resources. In short, the absence of a suitable family home in which to grow up.

José Ramón introduces him to Alicia, the social worker, Gloria and Alberto, educators, Luis, the support teacher, and María, who is in another area with the babies that regularly arrive. Lastly, the children he will have to help arrive; Nora, Edith, David and Santi. The four teenagers, between thirteen and fifteen, welcome the arrival of a young person to take responsibility for them.

At last, he is going to have the opportunity to help these kids, until there is another solution or, when they come of age, they can go to supervised flats, pursue academic studies, choose a profession, even find love. Except for the latter, Manuel considers himself lucky. However, his classmates, with whom he still has friendship, insist that he still has time to meet the right person.

One of the first afternoons, the juvenile prosecutor and a policeman come. Manuel seats Edith and then sits on a chair in the background, out of the immediate field of vision. After a couple of open questions from the policeman about her spare time and the friends she has made at the centre, the prosecutor intervenes:

"Edith, I'm David, the prosecutor for minors, and this is Jaime, a police officer. Do you know what a prosecutor does?" he asks. The girl denies, shaking her head.

"We try to learn what's happened to each of you. This interview is going to be videotaped. We need it this way to clarify some issues about your parents and about you. Do you agree?"

"I don't know what you want to know," replies Edith, agitated.

"Well, we're going to ask you some questions, but we want you to go beyond answering them and tell us everything you remember, what you don't, what you're worried about. We're here to help you" the policeman explains.

Edith looks for Manuel with her eyes, but he's already quietly gone. He will see the recorded interview later.

"Can you tell us what you did yesterday?"

"What I did yesterday?"

"Yes, give us as many details as you can."

"OK. I got up at half past seven, went to school and had maths, physics, language and English lessons. Then I went home with the educator and my partner Nora in the car. We ate macaroni. In the afternoon... we played dodgeball and then I went to school support, as always. I spent some time listening to music and... it got late. We had omelette for dinner, I watched an Eddy Murphy movie and... nothing else, I went to sleep," she concludes.

The experts suggest the topic of holidays. Edith remembers spending a lot of time at the pool and at a friend's house rehearsing dance steps, without even leaving Oropesa.

"Very good. Now we want you to tell us what you've come to talk to us about today," says the prosecutor.

She hesitates a little before starting, but, with the courage that characterizes her, she inhales deeply and decides to bite the bullet:

"I... I lived with my mother and Anthony. He was very mean, and he often yelled at her. I didn't get along with him, but I tried to keep out of trouble. He wanted to know what my mother was up to, what she was doing. If she was coming home from work, even if he arrived home hours later. He was also suspicious if she changed her clothes or stayed in her pyjamas. Sometimes he would hit her on the head and burn her with a cigarette. When he wasn't there, I would ask my mother to leave him," she pauses and then goes on talking with a choppy voice "but she didn't want to. I was about to report him, but she begged me not to. She said it would be worse and that he would be furious. He used to work as a driver... He'd spend a lot of time outside the house. He'd come back whenever he felt like it. Any attempt to ask him where he had been would make him violent. He'd get defensive, it was horrible. Sometimes he'd bring jewelry and it was like he was trying to buy her. We didn't know where he had got that kind of money. It was better not to ask him. Sometimes he'd spend hours ignoring her and not speaking, even days, so she'd feel bad and give in to something. To do what he wanted. If I tried to make him see reason, he'd send me to my room. One day I just couldn't put up with it. They were in the living room. They were screaming, I don't know what they were talking about. I heard... I heard them move and I got close to them.

He was grabbing her neck. I got in the way and grabbed him by the shoulders. I begged him to leave her. He yelled at me to shut up and told me I was a bitch. I didn't answer him, but..." she bursts into tears.

"Come on, you're doing great," says the prosecutor in a soft voice. "Can you tell us when that was?"

Edith pulls herself together and answers:

"I don't know, a few months ago. The days were endless."

"OK, now we want you to tell us what happened the day Anthony died."

"I... I was home alone with him. He told me that he would kill me if I ever interfered again. My mother... well, he hit her arms and legs a few more times. She denied it, but she had bruises. He wanted to humiliate me that day. He told me to pull down my pants and... he started touching himself!" she whimpers, bringing her hands to her face.

"What happened then?" the prosecutor insists.

Edith takes a deep breath, gets up her courage and goes on, this time without hesitation.

"My mother came in, grabbed him by the shoulders. She told him he was a pig, that he should be ashamed. Anthony turned around and punched her. He threw her to the ground. I saw my mother bleeding, so I took a sewing machine on the table and smashed it into his head. I didn't want to kill him! I didn't want to!" she sobs.

"Wait a moment, but that's not what your mother said" the policeman says.

"No, but she did it for me, to cover for me. I don't care if you take me to another facility. To a reform school. I have to pay for what I've done."

"Edith, we're convinced that it was involuntary. We'll talk to you and we'll always try to do what's best for you."

"Now we need you to tell us about Malory, your mother's friend, who died this summer. Did you know her?" the prosecutor inquires.

"I just knew that Sinead was her niece. I was acquainted with her, she was popular in the neighbourhood. All the older kids liked her. I saw Malory once when my mother was with her and she invited me to the fair, to the crazy cars. She seemed very nice," says Edith.

"Do you think Anthony could have killed her?" continues the prosecutor with his hands on the table.

"Hmm... I'm not sure, because they never talked about her. Anthony called someone the day before. I didn't catch the whole conversation, but I heard him say, "you have to do it tomorrow like we agreed. If you don't, you'll regret it.""

"This information is very useful. Do you have any suspicions about who he might have talked to?" the police officer asks.

"No, no idea. Anthony used to hang out with some bad people, maybe he sold drugs... Really, that's all I know."

"Thank you very much, Edith" both experts respond in unison.

CHAPTER XX

MANUEL OPENS THE apartment door and sets out to tell Brendan everything he's found out, but the other one acts first.

"Manuel, that in the hall is for you, it's been left in the mailbox," he says with a serious face. The Irishman's not due to get paid till next week, so he's not having a good day. The letter is from the court in Oropesa, which leaves Manuel totally unsettled. The boy opens it and begins to read it silently. The two of them remain standing.

"Can you tell me what it is and what you're supposed to do in Oropesa?" Brendan gets impatient.

"I worked as a lifeguard there a long time ago."

"And when were you planning on telling me?"

"Why? I was at the pool and serving as a socio-cultural entertainer at parties. I've been a monitor in many cities in Spain too."

"And you're the one who's going to help me? What are you hiding?" Brendan gets angry. He moves slowly towards him.

"Calm down, Brendan. Listen, they've caught Gerard with dirty money, and they want him to be a witness. He says they'll interview every worker he's had, that's all."

"So you know Gerard..." says Brendan, getting even closer.

"Of course, he owns the estate agent's business. Listen, I promise you I had nothing to do with it. I just want to help you. You realise I've asked to be assigned to that child protection center for that?

After a while, Manuel gets Brendan to settle down.

"And what did you find out, if I may ask?"

"Edith, I watched the video of her statement today. It says she killed Anthony unintentionally, trying to defend her mother. Apparently, he beat them both up and tried to abuse the daughter."

Brendan grimaces at her, between suspicious and excited.

"Wow, I knew that guy was hiding something."

"I mean, more importantly, Antony coerced someone on the phone the day before your wife died. We don't know what for."

"Who? Don't fuck with me!"

"Edith didn't even know. She just heard him say, "If you don't, there's gonna be trouble." I've got the interview saved. It's confidential, I can't disclose it, but if you promise me... "

"Cut the crap. We have to find out who's behind all this, who he threatened, if he was alone, and if Gerard..."

"Did you hear that? What's going on?"

A thud has just sounded in the balcony room. Brendan walks slowly through the living room until he reaches the bulkhead. He pulls the knob very slowly, slides the glass, and looks around him.

"What's going on," says Manuel from behind.

"Nothing, there's a lot of junk here. He must have moved something."

"What's that?!" Manuel screams.

"Oh no!" shouts Brendan.

A life-size inflatable doll has been placed at the box room, next to the washing machine. Brendan can't believe the appearance of the chilling grotesque figure. In its huge open ring-shaped mouth is embedded a plastic ice cube. The construction of the tongue and throat reveals knowledge of human anatomy. The author has spray-painted a blood stain on her belly, a detail which, added to the green eyes of that pleasure machine, inert and facing the infinite, chills his bones.

He runs backwards, collides with Manuel and falls to the ground, dropping a plastic chair and a bag full of history books, the ones Malory used to read. Is it the same person or, on the contrary, a joker without enough motivation or guts to commit a crime? Or maybe just a joker, or a group of kids who have made a bet? Is he warning of an imminent new attack?

Before he can react, a gloved hand hooks his foot tightly. The man is hooded, dressed completely in black. In the other hand he carries a knife with which he manages to prick him below the right knee. Brendan screams in pain and kicks him with his left leg. He manages to drop the knife on the floor, but the attacker has already held on to the bars of the balcony. Manuel is getting up from the ground, but the offender pounces on him and keeps him pinned down on his back. He punches him repeatedly in the face from top to bottom, until the floor fills with blood. Brendan runs to his aid and hits the man in the eye with the broom. He then kicks him in the ribs, knocks him down and takes the opportunity to remove his right glove. He touches his hand so that the fingerprints are impregnated, but when he prepares to remove the ski mask, the man punches him in the face again and finally jumps across the roof from the first floor before disappearing down a muddy path. Manuel remains stunned on the ground until Brendan cleans up his blood, helps him to sit up and gives him a glass of water.

Roberto and Rosa came at the request of the tenants and try to gather the scarce prints.

"We have some clues, but we must get more information to find out his identity," says Rosa.

"Where could the paint have been bought?" asks Roberto.

Brendan and Manuel wait while Rosa searches the database on her tablet. "The list of stores is so long that determining it is an even crazier idea than the fact itself," she says, tossing her hair.

"It's probably the same paint as the one on the patrol car," explains Roberto. Brendan mentions Anthony as a suspect of that act of vandalism and Manuel talks about Edith's testimony. Roberto notes all the details.

"I'm writing it down, although I'll soon be sent the video," he finally says.

Rosa and Roberto return to Oropesa. He drives, without exceeding the strictly permitted speed, almost all the way in silence, talking only about trivial things. When they park at the nearest gas station to the police headquarters, the lights are already on. Roberto stops to fill the tank and resumes driving.

"What's wrong with you?" asks Rosa as she sees his worried face.

"Nothing, it's just that all this is beyond me. We're stuck in this case and..."

"Roberto, we've had our ups and downs, but I want you to know that I'm going to do everything in my power to solve this case."

"Rosa, I don't know if Isabel has told you off... Don't take it personally, but you're not making any sense. Is everything all right?"

"Why do you say that?"

Roberto scowls and watches her carefully.

"What do you mean, why? You didn't give us all of Alex's calls. The video that Daniela had, we had to look for it ourselves because we didn't hear from you... Shall I go on?"

"I'm sorry, Roberto. I know I made mistakes. I was late. I've been very lonely lately. I have a lot of family problems, I sleep badly..."

"Please don't give me any excuses. You didn't find any more prints at the crime scene?"

"They mopped everything. We haven't been able to see anything else. We have to rule out everyone, the Gris company, Gerard and his subordinates, the lifeguard, the victim's friends... We'll solve it, I promise.

Roberto stares at her grieving face. He notices her expressive black eyes. She follows him with her eyes and kisses him gently on the lips.

Another night, by the town spa, now closed. The couples walk along the boulevard listening to the tourist entertainers give leaflets to the passers-by. Restaurants and attractions for the whole family: the water park, the performances at the tablao flamenco, the sports courts. At the end of the avenue, some children hum songs and wave balloons with their hands to the rhythm of two jovial clowns.

Without much deliberation, Rosa and Roberto choose the terrace with more room, responding to the call of the special cocktails they offer. The place is cozy; the music is quiet, instrumental.

Although there are some people seated, the atmosphere allows you to talk without having to raise your voice too much. Roberto notices the pleasant perfume of his companion.

"The blouse and earrings look great on you."

"Thank you."

The waiter takes their order and after five minutes brings a margarita for him and the classic mojito for her. The conversation goes from unimportant topics to her sentimental situation, aspect in which Rosa takes the initiative.

"I haven't had a partner for a year, I'm fine like this. What about you?"

"I'm unbearable. Nobody can stand me."

Suddenly, Roberto whispers something in her ear. In an oblique direction they observe another couple at one of the tables: Lidia and Fran. She's wearing a blue dress, quite a bit of make-up, and he's wearing a white shirt, Dockers trousers and black shoes.

The two police officers, very affectionate before, now show serious expressions. They scrutinize the young people without being noticed. After five minutes, Lidia and Fran ask for the bill and leave.

Rosa and Roberto finish their drinks and approach the magic garden, whose door, decorated with dragon motifs in relief, has been left ajar. The tourists stroll around the park and take pictures of themselves under the moon. The blue and green streetlights, worthy of a fairy tale, shine next to the trees, joined to stone benches, some of which are real, while others are sculptures with eyes and mouths that sometimes seem to move. The teenagers sitting there share cigarettes, laughter and confidences. In the centre, a Roman-inspired fountain stands out in front of a ceramic wall with a mosaic pattern formed by flowers and geometric figures.

From a wooden bench, they can see Lidia and Fran again. A man with a shaved head, wide features and long arms appears. He is probably Russian or Ukrainian. He watches from side to side and gives Lidia something that she quickly hides in her cleavage.

"Look, they're buying coke," says Roberto.

"Relax, you're not on duty" Rosa answers.

"But don't you realize that this guy could be involved?"

The agents walk quickly, but when they reach the end of the park, Lidia and Fran are already gone.

"Why don't we go to my house?" proposes Roberto.

"What do you think?"

* * * * *

ALREADY IN BED, Rosa crawls over to him. They intertwine their tongues gently, savouring each other's wet lips. Roberto grabs her by the waist, puts one hand down to her buttocks and caresses her crotch with the other. She slides her warm torso across his, letting herself fall into his arms. Breathing rapidly, Roberto runs his mouth down her neck and over her breasts until he hears her panting as well. Rosa arches backwards and he lowers his face on her belly. Then she places her legs on his shoulders and begins to swing back and forth. They end up embracing each other, looking at each other face to face, caught in a feeling of ecstasy.

CHAPTER XXI

ALMANZOR SIPS HIS black coffee while typing in a summary of Gerard's testimony.

"Tell me everything again to cross-check it with the report we got from UDEF, the economic crime report. So, you've run this brothel for six months, and in all that time you've never seen a fight."

"That's right, six, almost seven. There was no conflict at all."

"When you declare some of the money, did you say the girls were only massage therapists?"

"Exactly, actually that's what I authorize them to do."

"Well, from now on you're going to have to think of another scam, if I don't put you in jail. Are you kidding? You aren't telling me that all those ads you put on the internet were health-related, are you?"

"Inspector, I only opened the centre and hired the employees. I used to take a small commission, because the manager was in charge of the girls and the salaries had to be paid.

Gerard realizes he's cornered.

"But we have evidence that the figures don't add up. Much of it was laundered money Years ago you also took over that other slum, the Palm Trees nightclub, and some of those women didn't have a contract.

The promoter finally nods his head in agreement.

"Who obliged them?" "How many thugs did you have with you?" Almanzor curls his lips, giving him a sarcastic smile.

"Don't get confused, Inspector. No one ever forced them. We had a discotheque and hostel licence, and as for the guards, they did their job. I transferred the company."

"Because of disagreements with Vladimir, right? Come on, man, some were slaves who paid a debt. You set yourself apart after this girl died."

Almanzor shakes Gerard's arm hard and shows him Lisa's picture. Gerard recognizes her instantly.

"Yes, it was a client, but it didn't happen on the premises." The entrepreneur excuses himself.

"Sure, and do you know why? Because Daniela, one of his workers, ordered Adriana's husband to kill her to collect an insurance policy. They're all friends of Malory's. Don't you think there's too much death around you?"

"I don't know what you're talking about, sir."

The inspector ignores his answer and continues.

"Your wife is taking calls from the house they're in now. We know everything, Gerard."

Gerard nods the affirmative again.

"Who's the madam?"

"What does it matter?"

Almanzor makes an ironic gesture.

"Well, we have pictures of Eileen, the sister of a woman who was found dead in a hot tub at your facility, scandalizing dozens of residents and tourists and breaking the heart of her husband, family and friends. She opens the door to all those men and more!"

Gerard puts his head down.

"She left three days ago."

The inspector pounds the table with his fist, raising his voice.

"And who do you have in charge now? It was she who was there at the time when two clients had a fight. She tried to stop them, and a neighbour called here to the police station. But they had ran away.

"I have no idea about that. Eileen chose a new one, I gave her permission... This activity is not illegal. You can't condemn me. Hey, if you think I did something bad to those women, you're wrong."

Almanzor erupts into a sudden burst of laughter.

"You don't look like you're going around with a rifle, certainly, but you like money more than a fat kid loves cake. Well, what can you tell me about Johana Vélez Arango?"

Almanzor shows him a photo of Daniela's sister, to which Gerard responds with a chin quiver.

"Samantha for friends" the cop insists.

At that moment, Roberto opens the office door. Almanzor gestures his hand to stop talking, then tells him he can come in.

"Okay, I hired her to replace Eileen."

Almanzor gently pats him on the chest.

"So you're a liar too... Did you collaborate in her falsification of documents? Samantha had no job or papers; she kept her real surnames and changed her first name. It is likely that they planned some kind of trap: they invent sisters to commit frauds. It turns out that you sold a flat and exploited a woman in an irregular situation. Daniela disguised herself three years ago with a wig, contact lenses and fake skin, forced a man to commit a murder and then claimed compensation from the supposed death of that inexistent woman, using an identity card and a death certificate that someone had made for her. "

The Frenchman collapses and begins to cry.

"I didn't do it, I swear. I don't know what's wrong. This place is cursed. It's... it's been many years since we opened the resort. We sell flats and rent tourist apartments... in this and other areas. I wish, I wish this year could be erased from the calendar. But I, I can't be responsible for the fact that among the neighbours there are thieves and murderers."

"We are going to call all the employees you have had in the last few years as witnesses: lifeguards, cleaning and reception staff. You are facing a money-laundering offence. The penalty ranges from six months to six years, plus a fine of three times the value of the goods. Special disqualification from the exercise of your profession for a period of one to three years. If you are lucky, they'll close your bar and you'll have to find another job until further notice. Of course, we'll add another fine for pimping. But if we find out that you've been covering up a crime or have anything to do with it..."

"For God's sakes, Inspector."

Gerard makes as if to cross himself.

"Who do you know that are involved in all these operations? The mayor, some politician?"

Almanzor leans back in his seat and crosses his arms.

"What are you getting at? The mayor, yes, I have deals with him, but there's no catch. Everything was built according to his instructions, and with the expenditure items that I was told at the town hall."

"Gerard, I don't think we're going to get anywhere today. If you don't want to sing, you'll tell the judges what you know. Any information that comes to your attention, however small, you have the responsibility to pass on to us.

"All right, I will, I promise." Gerard says goodbye in a slightly childish voice.

During the interrogation, Roberto has simultaneously attended to what was said and to the documents on the desk.

"Jose, they're analyzing the prints. They'd left a bloody inflatable doll in the back room of Brendan's house. A hooded man appeared on the terrace with a knife."

Almanzor assimilates the hilarious story as he watches the officer. He is grateful that there is still someone, apart from his wife, who continues to call him by his first name.

"I couldn't speak to you more clearly because you were with Rosa. What I was trying to tell you was to stay away from her."

"But why?" asks Roberto, upset.

"What's wrong with you? Don't you see that Rosa is the one who has forged all those IDs?"

"What?!! But we don't have proof of that, Jose."

The inspector is holding his gaze. He notices a special gleam in his partner's eyes. "So you like her, eh, you bastard?"

Roberto blushes and looks down. "Why are you telling me this?"

"Well... I already knew... Let's see, I'll call Isabel right now. I've tracked down the date and the expedition team. The program gave me that data and we know it was her. She's done it for more people, apart from this case. She doesn't ask why they want it, she just charges for the work. It's the same as Gerard: as long as it's all on the economic front, suspension of employment and pay, penalty and that's all. The problem is that the documents he forges don't go to the best kind of people."

"How did you know that?" Roberto asks, perplexed.

Almanzor's expression contorts before answering.

"Know what? I know you. Look, do whatever you want, Roberto, but it can't be allowed. We'll take her off the case." He decides, patting him on the shoulder.

"Fuck off, Jose" responds Roberto, and they both laugh their heads off.

CHAPTER XXII

ALMANZOR HAS BROUGHT Isabel up to speed. The evidence that Rosa has falsified documentation is conclusive, but he needs to receive any information she can provide. The boss is puts her through to the specialist for the last time.

"Inspector Almanzor, I'm very sorry—"

"Rosa, we're in a hurry. Whose are the tracks of the man who jumped off the balcony?"

"The laser indicates that they belong to Anthony's brother, Ángel David Heredia." She pronounces every word slowly. "He has a record for drug trafficking. On a very small scale, a simple neighbourhood drug dealer. He acts with a gang of Russians who have already been convicted of theft and pimping. He's been arrested and says he did it as revenge."

"I understand."

"Forgive me for all the trouble I've caused. I was up to my ears with bills. I should never have accepted that money. I'll be disbarred, but I swear I've given you all the information I have."

"You don't respect the law because you're tempted to break it, or so I hope. If we find out you're hiding something else, I'll make you pay dearly for it."

"I promise, I've told you everything."

Almanzor hangs up without adding anything, looks at the clock on the wall and turns to Roberto.

"Come on, man, we gotta go."

* * * * *

Brendan parks outside the courthouse. Manuel gets out of the vehicle, nervous because it's the first time he faces a situation like this, even though he's only a witness. The guard, a gray-haired man wearing a cap, yellow shirt and black pants, smiles at him and asks him to wait.

"Are all these photos on the wall of missing persons?" Manuel asks.

"Exactly, young man. Many aren't found, but they always remain in our memory. You can enter now."

For a moment, Manuel remembers the kindness and affection he didn't receive from his parents, which eventually motivated him to want to help others. The guard's sympathy is diluted by the tension of entering the room. He looks at some familiar faces: the policeman who came to his house, the inspector who accompanies him, Gerard and a man with a moustache. On the right side of the room sits a group of young men whom he doesn't recognize. One of them, who they call Alex, answers questions from the prosecutor about his work that Manuel's brain can't process, because he feels like he's about to go bungee jumping.

"Manuel Jiménez Artero."

He notices his heart fast beating for no apparent reason. Although he has nothing to fear, his friendship with Brendan makes him want to get to the bottom of it. Perhaps the murderer is there, within these four walls, hiding behind the formalism of the legal proceedings.

"You worked at Helio Promotions between May and August 2015, is that correct?"

"Yes."

"Did you get a contract?"

"That's right, I was a full-time lifeguard and entertainer, 40 hours a week."

"What was your salary at the company?"

Manuel takes out the original documents and the photocopies, which he's brought along with the summons. "It was 840 Euros a month, net. Shall I give you the payroll?"

"Wait for the end of the procedure."

The prosecutor, known for his toughness in his profession, maintains his inquisitive attitude.

"Why did you leave the company?"

"My contract ran out."

"And you didn't work as an entertainer for a year? The elderly visitors support the complex in the off-season. Is there any reason why the company refused to keep you on?"

Manuel shrugs. "I don't think so."

"We know that you had a fight with a young man near the entrance to the apartment block, so the company decided to dispense with your services. Who was he?"

At that moment, Gerard and Alex look at him sideways.

"I don't think that's important. Who told you?"

"We're not here to answer your questions. Just answer mine. I'm telling you for the last time, who was the young man you hit?"

"A local boy."

"What's his name?"

"I don't know. I was dating a girl, then he came and assaulted me. He told me she was his girlfriend and to stay away from her."

"And you didn't try to find out anything else?"

"No, because I've never liked fights. The girl had told me she didn't have anything to do with him anymore, but that I should be careful. I spent some time working at another animation company and left town."

"She's called Marta?"

"Yes."

"How did you meet?" the official insists.

"In the neighbourhood."

"Did you know if any employees of the company Helio Promotions who were involved in crimes such as money laundering, document falsification or murder?"

"No."

"Did the company pay you all the money fairly, or did you receive any undeclared compensation?"

"No, it was all clean." Manuel repeats.

The statement has felt endless to him, but he is free at last. He hopes he never has to set foot in a place like that again. He doesn't know why he's been asked questions about his private life and what relevance they have to whether the Frenchman has stolen or killed a woman.

Suddenly, the mobile phone vibrates in his trouser pocket. Brendan's name appears on the screen.

"Brendan, where are you?

"How did the trial go?"

"Well, a bit tense."

"How's that?

"Because of the situation. I told them what I earned and when I worked here. Where are you?"

"Well, I'm here at a bar?"

"Where is it?"

"Wait, I'll send you my location. it's near the apartments, but closer to the highway. I didn't want to pass by that point, because I would have gotten sick."

"Okay, I'll come. See you later."

Manuel walks to the place. Four gentlemen are playing cards while drinking vermouth. Leaning against the bar, Brendan finishes his coffee.

"Do you have much left?"

From the kitchen, the waiter peeks through the bamboo curtain. Manuel notices how he stares at him and grimaces with distaste.

"Come on, come on, I'll wait for you outside" Manuel gets impatient.

"What's the hurry? Okay I'm going to pay and then we're leaving."

Manuel keeps an eye on the bartender, who's walking towards the beer shooters from the bottom of the bar. Before he gets there, Manuel exits without saying anything else.

CHAPTER XXIII

16 October 2018

"**A**LFONSO ZURBARÁN, DIRECTOR of the circus, approaches the microphone at the request of the judge. He is tall and ungainly, middle-aged, with a very striking black moustache and mid-length hair.

"At first, in June 2013, Oropesa's Smiley Face circus got off to a good start with some government support. It was 22 meters in diameter and 12 meters high, with stands, seats and a ring for approximately one hundred people, charging an entrance fee of 15 Euros. The speakers and lighting were contracted to Soundgail, as was the maintenance of the stage. We are currently working with the Gris company. I received the transfer of the tent together with the team of workers from Zaleski, a Russian businessman, to operate it during the summer months. In winter, the different shows take place in various parts of the country and I personally handle the hiring of staff for each campaign.

Although the beginning was expensive, little by little we managed to make some numbers very popular. In particular, the aerial acrobatic acts worked quite well, as did the activities with clowns and dance."

He seems to have learned all the speech by heart. The prosecutor lifts his head and sets out to ask a question:

"Is it true that you, your wife and your son used to stay in Gerard Briand's apartments?"

"That's right," answers Alfonso.

"How did you meet Mr. Gerard Briand?"

"He was my partner at the university."

"Did you receive any pay-offs from Mr. Briand?"

"Objection!" the defense counsel intervenes.

"Objection overruled," answers the judge.

"No, never." Alfonso testifies.

"Continue."

"Certain shows in particular were profitable for us. In time, the company's profitability began to decline, and the debt I had contracted with the Oropesa town council remained unpaid. We then expanded coverage, including all of Spain and coordinating our first events in France with an additional partner. All this is on our website.

"How do you explain the number of projects developed in cities like Barcelona, when your official profit and loss account shows much lower figures?"

Almanzor takes notes while Alfonso tries to justify the numbers.

"Did you ever sell drugs in your place in Oropesa?" continues the prosecutor.

"How? No, not at all."

"Mr. Zurbarán, the police and prison staff are aware that the Russian prisoners who kidnapped Brendan Sewan gave money from the sale of cocaine to his company. Was he the front man for Vladimir's gang? You will have to appear soon to testify in the trial for the death of Malory O'Dálaigh.

"They're lying."

"Are you suggesting they want to frame you for no reason?"

"Yes."

Almanzor knows the prosecutors' style. Coercive questions, which can only be answered in the affirmative or negative, in order to corner the opponent. As for Gerard, the accusations and proposals for sanctions accumulate; pimping, money laundering, influence peddling. When his turn comes again, he declares with courage and firmness, despite the unusual situation.

"As Mr Zurbarán said, the circus received a grant from the Oropesa town council."

"Did you put him in touch with the staff of the town hall?"

"Yes, with the one who was the mayor at the time, Mr. Raúl Vargas Ruiz, who is present in this room. I only did it to explain to him the process of public competition, to present the project of the circus within the framework of the leisure and entertainment offer of the town."

The mayor states the same as Gerard. The reasons for the mayor's resignation are divided between accusations of corruption and urban speculation, as well as complaints about inefficiency in the management of health and education by the opposition party.

Once at home, Almanzor receives a call from Manuel. As soon as he hangs up, the policeman returns to the courtroom to talk to the judge. All the assistants have left.

"OK, I'll get you a quick warrant if you find that the person is suspected of murder. I give you my word" the magistrate promises.

CHAPTER XXIV

Derek's phone is dead, so Almanzor decides to visit him directly. A group of children playing ball and two ladies are staring at him. He calls the intercom, but there's no answer either. The elevator has an 'Out-of-Order' sign, so he takes the stairs at a brisk pace up to the eighth floor. The door squeaks open and behind it he sees a woman who looks bad, almost rickety. She has lost all her head hair and much of her eyebrows.

"Morning, can I talk to Derek?"

"He's not in, what do you want?" the woman says in astonishment.

"I would like to ask him a few questions."

"Come in, come in. You know, he's gone with his father on an errand to the courthouse."

Almanzor is tempted to answer, "I know, I've just come from there", but he thinks it would be counterproductive.

"What's your name?" he stares at her thin ribs.

"Daphne," she says as she walks into the living room.

"You see, Daphne, we're investigating the death of a girl in a hot tub last summer and, well, we're asking the neighbours."

"Everybody?" the lady asks, upset.

The inspector hesitates before giving her an answer.

"The day she was murdered there were a lot of young people around the area; I know your son Derek works in a bar, so he probably has a lot of acquaintances and can help us find the culprit, if he's a local."

"Huh, right. In fact, if he's already out, he must be over there at the bar. I don't know if he was supposed to stop by and pick something up."

"And your husband?"

The woman looks at him suspiciously, wondering what he's up to. "He's been here a few days and has left. He said goodbye this morning, and after running his errand he left for Valladolid. He has a circus and travels a lot. My son is the one who takes care of me."

"Ah, yes, I've seen the tent they put up in the summer. Does your son look after you?" Almanzor repeats, hoping to get some additional information.

"I got breast cancer a long time ago. After two years without a trace of the disease, I felt my chest and noticed a lump. And I, of course, was scared. As much as I went to chemotherapy, the tumor spread. Eventually, they detected a metastasis that had reached my liver."

"Wow, I'm so sorry. Did you go back for treatment?"

"I went to the M.D. Anderson Center in Houston. Alfonso worked like a donkey all his life. When he didn't have any money, he went to his friend, the promoter, who lent him some, almost completely non-refundable."

"What promoter?"

"Gerard, don't you know him? The one from the real estate agency here."

"When did this happen?"

"Huh... I think 2015. Why are you asking me?

"No, no reason. How do you feel now?"

"Well, they had to treat me again, but I'm better now. I thought I'd never be cured."

"I'm glad. Excuse me, can I come in and look at Derek's room?

Daphne is suddenly suspicious.

"And what for, may I ask?"

"Don't worry, it'll be very quick. It's just routine, because we always fill out reports on the people we've been sent to visit. Pure bureaucracy, you know."

Daphne doesn't seem too convinced by the explanation, but she shrugs and accompanies Almanzor to the young man's room.

Almanzor's first impression is that Derek is a messy young man, but he has a lot of items. He has books of poetry and youth narrative all over the place. Among them are Baudelaire's *'Flowers of Evil,'* Rimbaud's *'A Season in Hell,'* Herman Hesse's *'Steppenwolf,'* and Fyodor Dostoyevsky's *'Crime and Punishment'*. In one of the drawers, covered with invoices, a photo of him with brunette girl. The two carry backpacks on their shoulders along a stony path. Underneath, a postcard split into several pieces. It's signed: "This is great. I'm learning the language of Asterix very quickly. I've seen the Louvre, Notre Dame and the Eiffel Tower. I hope you'll come with me next time. I love you. Martha." The desk is full of papers in piles that are held by pure miracle, notes from the institute and courses related to catering and tourism. On one of them there are telephone numbers that seem to have been copied from the address book, without thinking. Almanzor tucks the sheet of paper in his trouser pocket, takes a couple of pictures from the door and returns to the living room, where he finds Daphne sprawled out on the sofa.

"Very kind, thank you. Get better."

"Thanks to you."

When Almanzor takes the paper out of his pocket, he realizes he's seen that handwriting somewhere else. *"The threatening message they put in the car,"* he surmises. The running ink indicates that he's left-handed. Too bad there's no time to confirm it by further analysis of the strokes.

Almanzor runs to his vehicle and heads to the bar. The owner, puzzled by Derek's absence, tells him that the young man is a hard worker, and very punctual too. After a few failed attempts to contact him, the inspector rushes to phone Daphne to ask for Alfonso's number, which he has made the mistake of not getting.

"Alfonso Zurbarán? I'm Jose Javier Almanzor, Inspector of the National Police. I'm calling because we're trying to locate your son. He's not at home or in the bar."

"What? That's strange! He had a morning shift today."

"I know, I spoke to your wife, who gave me his cell phone, but it's turned off. "

"Did she call you?"

"I got a call from the bar." Almanzor lies.

"I'm on my way to Valladolid on business…Am I going back to Oropesa? – If you hear anything—"

Almanzor senses that the father is too quiet to know anything. He has one last call to make, but his battery is running low.

"Roberto, I need you to trace the phone I'm about to give you. It's from Derek, the bartender at the bar near the estate. Hurry up!"

The officer enters the coordinates into the computer.

"He's heading to the airport."

"I'm almost out of battery power. Follow the track on his mobile! Run! I'll wait for you there."

Roberto wonders what's going on, but he obeys without complaint.

Almanzor turns off the device during the journey. He turns it on when he arrives at the terminal, where he wanders around aimlessly. Roberto appears three minutes later.

"Boarding gate J40-J5, floor 1, Jose."

"Run!"

With bated breath, Almanzor tries to describe the waiter and his father. As he does so, he bumps into several angry tourists who don't hesitate to insult him.

In their frantic race, they make their way through the crowd climbing the escalators, shouting for permission. In the waiting room, a group of French people are waiting to board their flight to Paris, which is about to leave. Standing in a corner, Alfonso and Derek hug each other while the young man holds his boarding pass in his left hand, which gives him away.

"Derek and Alfonso Zurbarán," says Almanzor, under the watchful eye of the others.

CHAPTER XXV

BRENDAN'S DEFENSE ATTORNEY tells the court:

"Your Honour, Derek Zurbarán had a history of assault. Manuel Jiménez has stated that the defendant beat him up for going out with his ex-girlfriend, Marta — he looks at the girl, who nods, and continues his presentation—. Derek admits to having introduced dry ice in the private Jacuzzi the night before he knew that Brendan and Malory were staying at the resort. Dry ice is not toxic in itself, as is carbon monoxide, but carbon dioxide accumulated in excessive amounts can cause death, as it happened in this case. The lack of experience and access to that material, with the false alibi that it was for an event at the circus, makes it clear that to achieve it he resorted to his father, Mr. Alfonso Zurbarán, who should be punished for his complicity.

It has been shown that, on the morning of the crime, Lidia Rueda, a receptionist for the supplier company, limited herself to introducing this chemical into the pool in the usual amounts. Due to her short exposure to it, she only felt slightly dizzy, without blaming it on the ice, but Derek acted so in cold blood that he didn't care who died.

Mr. Zurbarán"s lawyer has indicated that there was no cruelty or treachery. However, the fact that Derek dumped the product obeying the now dead Anthony Heredia, who sought revenge for an infidelity and was also, according to the profile that has been made of him, a manipulative psychopath with a history of violent crimes, do not constitute mitigating factors for that the accusation of murder and not homicide be applied to him, since there is concurrence of price or reward.

Derek collected money that he actually invested in treating his mother's illness. However, evidence indicates that he kept a good part of the profit he made, which he completed working with small-scale cocaine trafficking, working for Vladimir Ivanov's gang, who is serving a prison sentence for trafficking women and drug smuggling, as he himself has just declared.

Mr. Ivanov was a partner of Gerard Briand. He betrayed him because he stole his businesses and 'his methods were enslaving and denigrating his victims', I quote verbatim what Mr. Briand told the Civil Guard. Derek wanted to hurt him by causing a crime in his urbanization. If he'd cared so much about his mother, he wouldn't have asked his father, Mr. Alfonso Zurbarán, to take him to the airport to flee to Paris.

As if that weren't enough, the analysis of his writing indicates that he tried to incriminate Alejandro, the lifeguard, who hasn't committed any type of crime; a poor man who worked honestly to raise his baby. Therefore, we are in front of a cold-blooded criminal, manipulative, liar and coward. He didn't care if he killed Brendan, Malory, or both, and if it hadn't worked, he would've tried other means.

Almanzor reflects on the lawyer's argument. *"Nothing is as simple as it seems, nor are there pure good or evil,"* he thinks as the judge firmly announces the guilty verdict. Perhaps Malory got dizzy from the concentration of the substance and collapsed. The blow to the head could have been what killed her. And Derek? Perhaps he had some plan to relocate his family elsewhere, to start over. In the notepad, the policeman notes that his demeanor throughout the procedure has been 'sad and crestfallen'.

Yaiza separates for a moment from her sister Marta to observe Sinead, who hugs and apologizes to Alex for having suspected him. Then Marta begins to scream desperately. Manuel runs to hug her, but she doesn't even look at him. Yaiza asks him to please walk away, clasping his palms together. He places his index finger on Marta's lips, puts his arm around her neck, and they both disappear without looking back. Eileen grabs Brendan's shoulders as they both cry, until he finally leaves the room with a random excuse.

"Do you want me to take you home?" Adriana asks him on the street. He takes her hand and smiles.

The next day, Adriana goes to the interview with Daphne.

"The tasks are cleaning, preparing food, running errands... Do you have experience as a caregiver?"

"Yes, I have worked with children for several years."

The woman seems close and affectionate. Adriana is convinced that she will soon regain her sanity.

At home, Sonia congratulates Almanzor while she prepares his folder.

"Congratulations. And good luck, professor."

"I'm already like you. What a waste of a person," he jokes.

"What else are you going to do, join Interpol?" Always protesting," says Sonia, as Izan pats her arm to wish her a good start in class.

From the podium Almanzor talks about instinct, passions, genetics, education, crime and other topics that, despite their lack of meaning, still fascinate him.

ABOUT THE AUTHOR

JORGE SÁNCHEZ LÓPEZ

Jorge Sánchez López was born in Madrid. He started to write poetry as a child, and came back to literature at the age of thirty. After training as a psychologist, he read English Studies in Spain. He has worked as a social pscyhologist, editor and training technician, and for some years he has been preparing teenage and adult students for Cambridge Exams at English Station, an academy located in Parla (Madrid). His published works include the poem books «Sentimientos o vasos comunicantes» (Andante, 2011), «Errática textura» (Celesta, 2013), «Aire y Ángeles» (translation of John Donne's poems for Celesta, 2015).   «Remontar la corriente» (Libros Indie, 2019) is his first book of collection stories, which has been widely acclaimed among Spanish readers. "Dry ice" is his first written crime and psychological thriller, which is coming out after « Nunca debiste atravesar esos parajes », a gripping FBI suspense novel set in Minnesota and Tennessee about the disappearance of several kids, was released by Seville-based publishing house Extravertida in 2020. He has also participated in local magazines and had a very active period in literary events of poetry and music in the Madrid scene, performing recitals with pianists and guitarists. His main focus is on stories which offer psychological tension and realism.